Prey and Predat
Part 2
American Isekai
By
Curtis Yost

PREY AND PREDATOR PART 2

First edition. September 15, 2023.

Copyright © 2023 Curtis Yost.

ISBN: 979-8223040033

Written by Curtis Yost.

Chapter 1

Isabella here. I'm just making a mild check to ensure you are up to date. Things are about to get a little wild so I don't want you confused. Here is a recap of the things that transpired in the first book. Just think back and remember.

I was born as Rachel Dawson. At the age of seven, Jacob Smith saved my life. The guy ran out in front of a bus to get me to safety and was crushed. I wasn't hurt bad, but it turned out that Jacob was a serial killer working as a paralegal. Jacob was able to see the victims easily with the help of a red-headed woman named Jamie.

I lost my parents on the same day due to two different scenarios. My mother was a bit of a slut and allowed strange men into our lives often. The one man went psycho and shot my dad to death trying to get to her. My mom was killed by an intruder in the house. She brought home a man that night who was about to rape me. I actually felt fortunate and unfortunate that the intruder showed up at the same time.

I ended up in the care of a loving family that did a television tour with me. James and Moira were excellent people. They both raised me the best that they could. It wasn't their fault that I became a serial killer myself.

James was a man who wrote books on the infamous Jacob Smith before people even knew who he was. The understanding was that he was a vigilante and protector of the weak. James never really saw my hero as a bad guy, but as a guy who felt compelled to protect the people around him. The average man would never stick their neck out to save someone. Jacob did it in the shadows. He did it for many years and lost his life saving his last child.

I was a typical teen girl until a worthless human being asked me on a date. He took me out for pizza and demanded sex. I kind of let him, so it wasn't all his fault. I ended up getting pregnant. When I told the guy that it was his, he denied me. The pain was bad enough that I poisoned him.

I lost the baby. The jerk's friends came over and beat the hell out of me. The internal bleeding was so bad that I was never able to have children again. There was a part of me that was grateful for having that done since I found my true purpose. Murder. The other part of me wished that I could have my baby boy to love and cherish. My life might have been a whole lot different and maybe would be still alive.

I killed a lot of people but was nowhere near as many as Jacob. My last place was at a house where two children were slain by their father. I was shot in the chest and bled to death. I was twenty-nine.

My body changed and I came across an angel named Angela. She claimed to be a buffer between God and myself. The angel was involved in my judgment that sent me to a second world that could be only dreamed up in fairy tales.

I was the second of eight children. I had an older sister named Matilda who didn't gain her skills until she turned fourteen. The girl was a miserable controlling cunt. I can't stand her, but Michael seems in love with her. I don't know what he sees.

I was a bit of a wild child who loved nature and the trees. I would climb every tree and jump around like it was nothing. I was this world's version of a tomboy and loved every minute of it.

On my ninth birthday, I saw my mother for the first time in eight years. I found out that I was half-elf. My ears were changing and I didn't like it. I had some really bad self-esteem issues when I found out what I was.

My mother was referred to as one the strongest Beast Tamers in the world. I was pretty much guaranteed a spot as a hero. The way I moved and reacted to nature. I knew that I was going to be a hunter and so did my father.

Once you realize that you are destined for something. You tend to avoid it like the plague. I didn't want to be a hero anymore. My royal status was high enough that I could still have a comfortable life.

I did get the hero status as a hunter against my will. My father was proud but had a weird feeling about him. He tried to treat me as an adult as my memories of my prior life came into effect. I was getting a rush of my old memories. The memories were causing me to lose sleep. Every night was having nightmares about my old life.

I even got a chance to see my old crush's life and found out that Jacob Smith was actually Michael in this world. I wasn't going to pass up this chance. Especially, since now, we are the same age. Jacob was my hero. But for some odd reason, he didn't act like I thought he would.

I was going through a personal hell trying to get him to notice me. At this point, I believe I came on too heavily so I was holding back a bit. He does know that I love him though.

When we were eleven, the three of us went on a mission to save a farm from bandits. Michael made short work of the bandits and killed most of them. An angel came to him and removed him from his body during the assault.

Lucas got in there and used weird spells that I hadn't seen before that moment. He was something else masquerading as a paladin. I saw him lift up men and suck all the blood out of their bodies worse than a vampire. I was freaked out, but the goal was accomplished and Lucas never did anything that would harm me.

Lucas and I managed to wake up Michael only to discover that he was with his angel the whole time. There seemed to be something eerie about the whole thing as Michael smiled while he was talking about the experience.

We later tagged along with my sister and got her the blessing of an Elemental Mage. She might not have lived if Michael didn't stand up to her as the church was going to kill her. Also, our new group members Paine and Loraine were there. I thought they would be funnier since they had alike-sounding names. They were not.

A couple of days later, Lucas and Michael's father, James, were killed by an evil Warlock named Gandriel. I spent most of the time with Lucas's girlfriend and baby mama Marcy.

Marcy was a powerful barbarian who battled Lucas and Michael during our guild initiations. She beat Lucas but lost to Michael only because he was so fast that he couldn't be seen.

After the attack on our family, a war strategy was put into place. We had to kill the king, Norman. I still get a kick out of the fact his real name was Norman. He hated it so bad that he would only let people refer to him as the king.

The pieces were set and we brought on Paine and Loraine to take down the king. The group got together and we took down the guards. The place was a mess. I couldn't stand it.

Matilda and I didn't want to get splattered by blood. So we walked to the king's location. The walk there was rough. I really wanted levitation or at least something to get me up the steps.

Matilda and I witnessed him rape a thirteen-year-old girl and kill her brother. The shock was devastating. I wanted to help the young girl, but knew that his end was near, and couldn't do anything yet.

After the warlock's death, Paine came to us. He was covered in blood and so was Loraine. The blood slid off of him because of what the armor was made of. Loraine was drenched from head to toe in blood. She didn't look happy about it.

Michael came up after he was finished with the girl and slaughtered all the king's men. He attacked the king and killed him mercilessly over a thousand times. The king kept resurrecting because of some diamond that he had in the room. The power of the diamond was completely depleted and the king finally died.

Michael transformed into a vile beast that was more demon than man. He had horns and scales. I found it oddly attractive, but knew he needed to be stopped. After the death of the king, he tried to attack us.

Paine opened a portal dragging him in and came moments later. Michael was completely knocked out and looked like his horns were ripped off. I was just glad to see he was back to normal, but that forceful raw power. I don't know. It was kind of a turn on in a way.

We went to the church on a random night and got him blessed. That was a new development. The blessing sealed the demons into his body and gave him absolute control over them.

The next day a parade for the king's son was coming through town. Michael missed one and this guy was more vile than his father from what we were told. The group was plotting the guy's death until the girl that Norman fucked saw him. She hid a knife on her. The guy didn't care and thought she was cute so he let her onto his mobile throne. I guess you could call it. There were two girls on there already and didn't think the guys carrying him would mind.

The girl stabbed him with the knife. Since the men carrying him weren't focused on the throne. She stabbed him throughout the parade. The guards weren't paying attention and just noticed the cheering from the crowd. My father was now the king and I was a princess. That just feels weird to say. Especially since I'm part elf.

We went to the Reaper guild and got a new assignment that had our names on it. A man named David asked for us to find a group of missing women who were being kidnapped by goblins and taken back to be breeders.

The group went south through the forest where things seemed peaceful for the most part. When we saw the sand past the forest. The group took a moment to actually get to know one another. There were some odd exchanges, but the main thing we got out of it was that Paine is messed up from his childhood and doesn't want any children.

Paine took the reigns and I sat on the roof looking over the landscape and kept a close eye on the Hyenas. They were my friends and puppies. I had a close spiritual bond with them and they were loyal to me.

A wyrm appeared in the distance and chased us into a sandstorm. I attacked the wyrm with a strong Fire Arrow spell. The wyrm left us alone, but Paine drove us into the storm. The desert was like a hurricane. I got tossed into the air above the clouds and was dropped into the sand. I was sunk in.

A group of goblins saw I was alive. I was barely able to move. Some of the goblins were five times the size of a human. I believe they were called hobgoblins. I was carried by one of those until we reached a point. The goblins built a campsite for us to rest.

At that moment, I saw a young girl who was in my shoes. Her family was killed and she abandoned all hope. I told her that we were about to get out and just needed some time.

The girl's name was Delilah and believed I would save her. She was preparing to escape, but we were dragged back to the breeding grounds. We watched as other girls were being raped by the goblins.

Delilah and I were in the cage waiting for our impending doom. I turned on my camouflage hoping to never be seen as my babies were going to direct the group to our location. There is a spiritual bond that forever connects me to the hyenas. Sylvia stayed with them and Diego stayed with me.

This was the beginning of the Goblin War.

Chapter 2

I sat there staring at the goblins as they were raping poor Delilah. I wanted to do something, but I had no arrows, no bow, and no knives. I was defenseless at the moment.

The goblins were taking turns inseminating here. It was as if that was their only purpose in life. This was how the race was surviving. I watched and noticed that I didn't see a single female goblin in the bunch.

The goblins were wearing brown loin clothes. The limited clothes made it easier for them to get into action immediately. The place felt like a weird ritualistic cult. They were like hive-minded animals that only knew how to destroy.

I could smell the pungent stench of blood and semen coming from the goblins. Their sinister sexual urges were making the dungeon gross as they would assault their victims and each other.

The bars were black and rusted. The moistness in the air was corroding them. The bars were flaking off into the air if you touch them. When the goblins opened the door. They would get what looked like green soot on their hands.

The ground was made of stone. It felt like a cave that was carved out for torture chambers. The floor flickered like a rainbow was on them. It glistened from the light of the torch flames.

Water was dropping from the ceiling and hitting the floor. The constant sound from it was deafening. I couldn't stand it anymore. Between the women screaming constantly from giving birth to more goblins, or the constant sexual assaults. I couldn't stand it anymore!

I stayed strong for my faith team in my team was helping me gain endless hope. I just had to keep up my camouflage for as long as I could. There were moments, when I could feel it fading. If I kept my strength up, I was sure that I could keep it up for a total of fifteen days.

The problem is that I need water and food. The lack of sustenance was making me feel weak. I needed my strength to keep Camouflage up. My stomach was aching from hunger. All that went through my mind under control was to remember the good times to keep up my morale.

My Camouflage was keeping up in this dreary dark place. The obstacles of hungry and not giving up were far from easy. When I was having issues with keeping my Camouflage up, Diego would take over. He was my knight in shining armor.

Since the goblins only brought enough food for Delilah. I could not take it from her. She was losing so much nutrition from being pregnant all the time. I could not bring myself to steal from her.

The goblins would walk down the corridor like clockwork. I could time them like a cheap watch. The goblins were like drones that were completely controlled. The only reason they were a threat at all was their numbers.

I had an ability that could get me out of these chambers but didn't have the weapons to kill with. I watched and waited to see who had what weapon to see what was the most effective. A few goblins had rusted swords on them, but most had clubs.

The large doors in the front that were hard to open. The doors required the strength of at least four hobgoblins. I never had the strength open the doors by myself. Michael would find a way. He always pulled amazing amounts of strength out of nowhere.

The doors reminded me of some of the dungeons we did growing up. The fresh air when we got outside. The moment we finished gave me a wonderful feeling of freedom. To keep my mind off of things around me, I remembered our first dungeon. I still feel bad about this.

Michael, Lucas, and I were ten years old. We got a dungeon quest from the guild. Apparently, the dungeon was small, but heroes kept dying from it. My father, who was training me the whole time was pointing out how using my skills on a real dungeon. Might be the best thing for me.

I was outside a village called Tameron. Tameron was a small village of about two thousand people. The dungeon was their commerce. These were good, hard working people that were weird because they lived nowhere near civilization.

The three of us got to the village. The roofs had hay on them. The buildings were like that of log cabins. I could see kids peeking out the windows. The road going in had a welcoming sign.

Every house had flowers on the front. There were many merchants for food and gear. They had things available for the travelers. Apparently, there was something about this dungeon that kept killing all the adventurers.

The people tried to make an honest living from reselling the items from the dead heroes. Some of the people knew the starter traps and would retrieve the items. The strangest gear was the ones that smelled like shit. That was a weird one for me.

I often wondered if he people in the town managed to kill the heroes. Some of the looks were got were sinister in nature, but nothing became of it. There was no proof that any of the villagers caused harm.

As we walked into the town a young blonde haired girl with a green dress came up to me to buy some flowers. The outside of the town was full of them. The fresh air blew the flowers fragrance throughout the town. I just simply told the young girl I didn't want one.

I asked the young girl, "Do you know where we can get a bite to eat?"

The young girl pointed to door about three buildings down and to the right. The building had a weird symbol on the front of it. It was clearly a tavern, but the little girl that tried to sell me the flowers had the same symbol on her dress.

A young boy yelled the word "two." Michael got hit in the face with a wooden ball. I think the kid meant four. The ball bounced off of Michael as if he never had a brain.

Michael wasn't wearing his demon gear. So the full brunt of the hit got him. I could tell that he was hurting a bit. There was a mark on his forehead that told me he should be knocked out.

Despite the fact that he looked severely harmed. The blow barely phased him as he just looked around trying to figure out where it came from. The force of the hit had the townspeople watching us in shock.

The gargoyles Michael was collecting were making his skin harder. He was also losing control of them as they would sometimes hold back from doing what he wanted to do. In most cases, I would agree with the gargoyles. Michael was kind of an idiot who made decisions on a whim.

The boy who hit the ball said, "Sorry, mister."

Michael just smiled at him. He couldn't possibly be mad at the child for a simple mistake. Unfortunately, he bled a little and the townspeople noticed. Purple blood was the sign of a demon. He was only half-demon, but they are the most feared creatures in the world. You can't tell the difference between the two species.

The mother of the boy ran out and kept bowing and apologizing. Michael kept moving his hand up and down. Michael said, "It's quite alright. I'm perfectly fine. No harm no foul."

Michael was larger than a normal kid at this point. He had a soft side for children. He would always go out of his way to soften his voice whenever talking to one. It didn't help the situation at all because they knew what he was.

Michael took his left hand and wiped the blood away. His face was as good as new. I could see him trying to gauge the place. Something felt really off. He didn't know who these people really were but felt like that was no accident.

We walked down to the local tavern and sat at a table. I smelled the food. It was a simple stew with fresh vegetables and a little bit of beef. The cooks said it was complementary since we were new to the town. Nothing in this world is free.

The bowls were given to each of us. I didn't smell or see any poison effects. All I could do was watch as the other two ate the soup. I asked them if I could have a fresh salad with no meat in it.

Michael said, "What are you a rabbit now?"

Michael had a grin on his face thinking he was funny. Michael looked at Lucas and raised his eyebrows at him.

Lucas looked at him and said, "Don't bring me into this."

I ate the salad and gave Michael my food. He really liked the soup. I wasn't sure if I could trust it, but with his healing abilities the man would only get stronger if it was poisoned. If anything, I believe the people would try to kill us since our companion was a demon.

I looked around the building. It was very small. The building had wooden planks that would pop up a little when you stepped on a certain spot. It made me think that there was something hidden underneath the floorboards.

The lights had one chandelier with candlesticks in them. During the day there were several windows to keep the place bright. The heat from the sun was making everything warm. I just wanted to get out as I was feeling sick from the heat.

Michael's eye started to twitch a bit. This was the moment that I realized they poisoned the soup, but not intentionally. The reason the soup was free was because they wanted to use the meat before it turned. The gesture was kind, but the outcome was not.

Michael asked, "Where are your bathrooms?"

The bartender said, "There is an outhouse out back."

Michael moved fast to the outhouse. Something got to him. His eyes started to glow purple again as he ran out the front door. The bartender thought the way he moved was really rude. I could see a scowl on his face like we did something wrong. I paid for our drink and food and walked out after him.

Lucas and I got to the outhouse and knocked on the door. Michael said, "I'm in here. Just give me a min...AAAHHHHHH."

I asked, "Are you okay in there?"

Michael responded, "I am just releasing the demons. I think there was something wrong with the soup."

Lucas thought it was hilarious. He used a Heal himself after realizing there was something wrong with the soup. There was one problem. Heal didn't cure him from the poison. I could hear his stomach rumbling hard. His face was looking green.

Lucas realizing the only outhouse around was preoccupied by his best friend ran into the field. He stripped off his armor leggings and dropped his knees into a squatting position. Lucas in all his glory was grunting in the middle of the field. The stench from his crapping was so potent that it killed the wonderful fragrance of the flowers. Now it had a weird smell like orchids and shit.

The townspeople came to check on what was making that awful smell. Lucas just kept crying out, "Don't look at me! Don't look at me." Followed by a small whimper.

The two of them were stuck there for three hours. I was waiting for the townspeople to attack us with pitchforks and torches. I was just grateful that I didn't eat the soup. My mind was set on getting us rooms. The boys could share and I would get my own. A part of me was thinking of sharing with Michael and maybe putting the moves on him, but after that smelly display. I knew that I had to pass.

I slept in my own room next to theirs. There were four rooms in the whole inn. Three of them were upstairs. I'm guessing not a whole lot of people come out here except heroes looking for a quick buck.

I looked out the window and saw the stars filling the sky. The quiet and the visuals were amazing. I would like to say that the flower smell came back, but these two idiots ruined that for everyone. I can still taste it in my mouth.

I lay in bed and closed my eyes. The guys were in the room next door. I was trying to sleep, but Lucas was making orgasm noises. It was really hard to take hearing your brother make slapping noises and going OOOOOOOOOOHHHHH! I did my best, but it was too late. I visualized my brother's O face.

The town was dark. You would think that those two would want to get some sleep. The next thing I hear was Michael yelling, "Watch, kick me in fucking nuts!"

I used the pillow and pushed it over my ears. I tried to drown out the noise the best I could. The problem was that I was literally the only girl on the mission. I couldn't stand it anymore.

I pounded on the door and told them to shut the fuck up. Michael said, "We are trouble. I hope she doesn't sick those Weiner dogs on me."

I put my face on the pillow and screamed. Men were the bane of my existence. I swear. Their juvenile behavior only made the mission harder for me. Especially, since I'm in love with one of them and was asking myself. Why?

The sun rose and I got maybe three hours of sleep. My hair was everywhere and looked like I stuck my tongue in a light socket. My hair needed to be combed badly, but didn't have any of the slaves to help me with it. I just sat there on the bed trying to blow it out of my face.

In the world, I had no girlfriends to talk too. I thought about how Mercedi and I would talk about the issues in my life. I really don't have that now. I mean, who in my life could I depend on to talk to. My sister, Matilda, would find a way to use anything against me. Jasmine maybe. That sister was in her own world.

The building was hot so I slept in the nude. I jumped to the floor and put on my clothes real quick before Michael flew in my window or something. Once,

I got my clothes on. I used X-ray to see into their room. I wanted to see if they were awake yet.

Michael was awake and not wearing any clothes. It looked like he was brushing his teeth. I have no idea where he got the toothbrush since he didn't have one traveling here. I went over to their room and knocked on the door.

Lucas and Michael just flung open the door and stood there naked. Lucas said, "Come in. I don't want strangers to see us naked."

I said, "Why do you think it's okay for me to see you naked."

Lucas responded, "Because you're you know....you."

I wasn't sure what the hell that meant. I was still a girl after all and a young one at that. I couldn't be caught in a room with two naked young men. Even if one of them had incredible muscles and didn't mind watching. I blushed at the thought of it.

Michael spit the toothpaste out and said, "Did I ever tell you about the time I was tea-bagged by an albino bear."

I said, "Yeah like a hundred times now."

Michael claimed that he was tea-bagged by an albino bear. A tea-bagging is when a person or thing drops their nuts on you. You have to be bareballed for it to happen. At least, I think you do.

Anyway, we had cat people out there watching him the whole time and they claim that if a bear actually did come out. They would have slaughtered it before the bear had a chance to bite him in the first place. Everyone thinks he hallucinated it. Even Paine admitted that it probably never happened and he never knew him then.

The guys got around and we headed to the dining area to be fed. I was planning to eat just bread. Lucas and Michael were asking themselves if they should risk the mission and get breakfast.

Michael said, "Fuck it. I'll have bacon and eggs."

The caretaker replied, "We are making you bread and giving you bananas. There is no way your stomachs will touch meat around here again."

That had to be humiliating. The boys had a reputation now for not being able to handle meat. I believe the people of the town were just used to it and their bodies adapted. Since my father froze his food with mages. This rarely happened.

As we ate, Diego and Sylvia came to my feet and rubbed up against my legs. I miss them being so tiny. The spirits would often lay dormant in their bodies to keep them under control. I could feel their presence at all times, but they didn't say much.

Afterward, I asked the innkeeper, "Do you have any advice for the dungeon?"

The innkeeper said, "We have a dungeon specialist in town. He buys and sells all kinds of gadgets to help travelers. He is in fact the most knowledgably right up to the labyrinth. I'm sure he will set you on the right path for a price."

Lucas, Michael, and I walked a few houses down to a shop that matched the innkeeper's description. The house was made of stone and had a solid sheetrock foundation. The sheetrock was covered in hay so as not to let water get inside.

The outside has large traps. I would say bear traps normally, but they were four times the size of that. How the hell would you carry that stupid thing into a dungeon. The dang thing snaps and collapses the dungeon.

We walked into the store and the floor was made of stone. Behind the counter was a staircase to the basement. The man had a home designed to fortify him from the rest of the world. I looked through the floor and saw so much food that I believed he had a family of fifteen.

I asked, "How are you today, sir?"

The guy replied, "What do you want?"

The man wasn't the friendliest of people and showed no signs of having a wife or children. I think he prepared all that food for himself. The man was waiting for the end of the world. I was trying not to pry as there was a possibility that his man was completely crazy.

I said, "We are looking for equipment and advice for the dungeon."

The shopkeeper said, "If you want my advice when you enter. You should stick your head between your legs and kiss your ass goodbye."

I was thinking this was rather rude. The guys were looking at him like they were taking notes. They didn't catch on that he meant we were going to die. I could see Michael trying to see if he was able to do it for the dungeon. I just shook my head.

I asked, "What for wares do you have?"

The man said, "What you see is what you get."

I looked around the room and saw a few shitty weapons, rusted traps that looked used, and a large bucket of metal rods. The rods seemed to be weirdly shaped with a hook on the end. I walked over and looked at the rods. One end was rusted and had a weird shape on the tip, and the other side was clean, black, and didn't have a scratch on it. I picked one up and touched the tip of it. It seemed dull and smelled a bit.

I asked, "What does this rod do?"

The shopkeeper said, "You shove it up a large monster's ass. Maybe swish it around a bit."

I immediately dropped the rod on the ground. That was gross. I had just touched monster shit. He could have at least cleaned it before reselling it. I realized that nothing in this place worked. The shopkeeper would go in and retrieve the items for resale.

I said, "Let's go guys."

Michael replied, "But what if we need to ram a dragon in the ass. I mean that might be the one way to kill it."

I shook my head in disgust. Michael was actually believing in this nonsense. An iron rod wouldn't do anything, but get someone killed. Obviously, other heroes like Michael tried. Heroes that didn't have a good grasp on reality and died for their troubles.

Michael bought the rod anyway from the merchant. I just shook my head. Two silver for a metal rod. That was highway robbery. I really hope he didn't believe in the rod and was just being courteous to the shopkeeper.

We walked out the door and Michael was swinging the rod over his head. If he gets a single piece of shit on me. The dungeon won't have to kill him. I'll kill him instead. It really was kind of funny watching him try to wield a rod that he didn't know how to use at all. He hit himself in the head a few times. A small piece of crap got lodged in his hair like a dingleberry.

Lucas, Michael, and I, all left the village to go to the top of a steep hill. I was afraid to slip and roll down the hill. My mind was getting the better of me. The hyenas were using their claws to dig into the ground. Lucas put his shield on his back and used the sword to pull him up like a walking stick.

Michael, I hated him at that moment. He used the shit stick to pull himself up the hill. The ground as we got closer to the top of the hill had a weird methane smell. The ground was moist. I was in my bare feet. I was feeling really gross.

Michael said, "I think that is troll shit. There might be a troll somewhere around here."

My head and body shook really hard. I was going to throw up. I had no choice though but to trudge on. The squishiness in my toes was not helping at all. Michael looked over at me and smiled. I wanted to kill him, but that was just the stress making me feel that way.

We got to the top of the hill in front of the dungeon. I sat down in a dry spot and took out my water vessel to drink. Lucas sat beside me.

Michael said, "Let me go in first you guys can rest."

Chapter 3

Lucas and I sat there drinking water looking over the field and sky. The view was amazing. We could barely see the people in the village. The children were playing in the streets. The flowers were overtaking the smell of troll shit. The place seemed magical in a way.

Michael walked over to the gate and pushed on it. The door wasn't opening at all. He was trying to get inside but was failing since the door required more strength. His grunting noises while trying to push the door were really starting to irritate me.

I walked over and looked at the gate. There were two handles on the door. The door was wooden with a metal frame. The size of the doors had to be fifteen feet high. It had carvings written on the door handles. I would say the markings looked goblin.

I asked him, "Did you try pulling the door?"

Michael grabbed the handle and it came right open. I walked back about seven feet and sat down. I had to see what he was going to do. The place was described as a labyrinth. How was he going to do this without my expertise? I had Scan and X-ray which are some of the most important skills for dungeon crawling.

Michael bent over and touched his knees and walked forward. I was thinking, "What the hell is he doing?!" I realized he was taking the words from the shopkeeper and was sticking his head between his legs to kiss his ass goodbye.

I was about to say something, but a blade came across and swiped above his body. The blade continued to spin and go back and forth. Michael formed two swords and sliced the arm on the blade dropping the blade to the ground.

Michael got a huge grin on his face. I could see that look of cockiness. He was about to run the whole dungeon. Michael was going to set off every trap in the place intentionally so that we could run it safely.

Michael's eyes turned purple with a spark coming off of them. His purple hair was sticking up into the air like a cartoon. Purple lightning was coming off of his body and off he went into the dungeon. All I could hear was traps echoing throughout the cave. This dungeon was going to be cleared by an amateur only because he was faster than the traps.

I walked over to Lucas and sat down. I said, "So how is life treating you."

Lucas replied, "I think I'm finally wearing down Marcy. She has been laughing at me a little more lately. I just turn on the old Lucas charm and she becomes putty in my hands. I spend most days now trying to think of ways to make her laugh."

I honestly think they make a great pair. He was abandoned by his parents. I guess his father was a paladin close to the church. The man was high-ranking and didn't want anything to do with him. The church told him that his father died valiantly against an evil mage when he was three.

Lucas had an image of what his father was in his head. He was like a white knight who would always save the women of the castle. He believed that his father always ran into battle and defended the kingdom against many foes. I later learned from Paine was really happened. I feel bad for the guy. Luckily, he is nothing like his father.

Lucas said, "How about you? What is going on with you."

I replied, "We live together what do you mean."

Lucas had a grin on his face. He was trying to get a feel for Michael and my relationship. I wasn't sure what to tell him in case he blabbed something stupid to his best friend in the whole world.

Lucas asked, "Your relationship with Michael. Where is it going?"

I replied, "Michael wants nothing to do with me in that way. He wants Matilda. To be honest, I'm not sure I want him. He is impulsive and rude. He does things that make me want to throw up all the time. Michael doesn't think before he acts and insults me all the time. We are both adults and he acts like a child all the time."

Lucas questioned what I was saying, "Are we adults? Ten-year-olds are adults? I mean we aren't exactly sure what parts of us are from the old world and what parts stayed there. In this world, I suffered but found happiness much later in life. My past life was nothing but suffering. I'm not going to let being an adult get in the way of living life to the fullest. Also, he finds Matilda to be beautiful, but he likes you more. I rarely hear him mention our sister's name. You have his heart, even if he doesn't recognize it yet."

I said, "Thanks. I think I needed that."

Lucas replied, "No problem. That's what big brothers are for."

I rebutted, "I'm three days older than you."

Lucas looked at her and just smiled. He always thought of me as a little sister. Since the first day we met, he thought of me as family. It was one of the things that made him who he was. He found power in family. Even if it wasn't family by blood.

I closed my eyes and tried to get a wink of sleep, but the ground began to shake. I got up and looked into the dungeon. Michael popped out in front of me and pulled me to the side of the cave. He put his pointer finger on his lips and made a shushing sound.

I had my back against the stone on the outside of the dungeon. The ground was shaking even worse than before. The rumbling was clanging the armor on Lucas. Michael jumped on top of him to reduce the noise.

Lucas said, "I'm not into dudes still."

Michael had a look of shut up. That serious look that Michael didn't have most of the time made me feel uneasy. It was also a little bit of a turn-on. I kind of liked it when he acted tough and had a leader mentality.

I heard a crashing of the doors in the front of the cave. A large twenty-foot boulder ripped through the entrance and blasted off the doors. Rocks flew everywhere and Michael got on top of me. His first reaction was to act like a shield for me.

Michael put his armor on and let the rocks hit his back. I think he was afraid of burning me with the front of his armor. He got hit was six big rocks and a crazy amount of debris. I wanted to help him, but I was only an attack type at the moment.

I was hot at that point. My ears began to tingle. Michael was lying on top of me. He embraced me so well that I never wanted this moment to end. At that moment, if he were to kiss me. I would have been his for the rest of my life.

Michael said, "Sorry, I got a little wood. It happens if I lay on any girl."

The mood was gone. He blew his chances. I pushed him off of me and just wanted to get away. I was an emotional wreck at that moment. I felt a pain in my chest and wanted to just... punch him I guess.

Another boulder rolled out of the dungeon and flew down to the village. The rocks were tracking something and attacked the village. I could hear the sounds of screaming as the people were trying to run away from the boulders. It was as if the boulders had a life of their own.

Three more boulders popped out and flew down the side of a hill to the village. I looked over at Michael. He just smiled at me and shrugged his shoulders. He stood up removing his armor. Michael brushed off the black shorts that he wore after Wong convinced him they were the best for someone like him.

I asked, "What the fuck did you do?!"

Michael said, "I might have set off traps in the maze that had heat-seeking boulders. They were slow, but I had to escape since I almost got crushed a few times."

I said, "Why didn't you just destroy the boulders."

Michael replied, "There is no way for me to destroy them."

I looked at him in such a way that he realized he messed up. It was like he didn't realize his own move set. Michael had one of the strongest moves in his world and he didn't bother to use it on a boulder.

Michael continued, "Since you have the fire thing used at the stadium. I figured you could destroy them. I have no moves designed to destroy large objects like you."

I looked at Lucas and he said, "Don't look at me. I'm mainly defensive and my sword wouldn't cut through the boulder."

The screaming from the people in the village was piercing even at this height. I even heard someone say, "For the love of God, why is this happening. This never happened before."

I scanned down there and saw the children were the first to be killed. They just weren't fast enough to evade the boulders. The Inn we stayed in was smashed to pieces. Luckily we packed light and didn't leave anything in there.

I looked at Michael and said, "Why didn't you use Sonic Slice? That should have done the trick."

Sonic Slice was a move that allowed him to use sonic vibrations and cut through anything. He even had a way to toss the sonic vibrations at a foe cutting them in half. I figured he rarely used it because it took a lot out of him, but it seems he just completely forgot he had it.

Michael looked at me sheepishly and said, "Oops."

We stood with our arms crossed watching the village be demolished by sentient boulders with an attitude. I witnessed one of the boulders on top of an eighty-year-old woman. It just kept bouncing up and down like an African Jumping Bean. The boulder killed her and kept continuing to jump on her to add insult to injury.

The townspeople were bringing out all the stops with their weapons, but since not a single person there was a hero. The people didn't stand a chance. Everything was crashing down and homes were set on fire while the boulders crashed through them.

I looked at Michael and exclaimed, "See what you did!"

Michael asked, "What can I do now? I thought they would stay in the dungeon."

Lucas said, "The boulders may return after the village is destroyed. We should be vigilant. I believe you will have to destroy them, Michael."

Michael asked, "And what are you going to do."

Lucas said, "Protect our hunter who is probably the only person here able to get through the labyrinth."

Michael nodded his head and stood in front of the dungeon waiting for the boulders to return. He was so fast that I thought he would just rush down there and slash the boulders, but instead just sat there waiting for his turn when the townspeople were all dead. I wasn't sure how to ask him to defend them, but instead left him be.

After everything down there was smashed every living thing, even the roaches were killed. The boulders came up to us. The boulders noticed us standing there waiting and sped up the hill as fast as they could. They moved fast through the spots where the local troll was shitting. The boulder were saturated in crap. The cracks on them had crap caught in between.

As the boulders got up towards us slipping a bit from the wet ground and shit. Michael wound up, and threw several Sonic Slices at the boulders completely destroying them. The blast hit so hard debris and shit was flying everywhere. There was shit everywhere and not a dang thing I could do about it.

Michael just stood there as the stone, dirt, blood, and shit fell from the sky onto us. I couldn't be mad. He did exactly what I told him to do, but it doesn't mean I had to like the fact that he just covered me in blood and shit.

Once the debris stopped falling from the sky, Michael said, "Let's go in family." With a smile on his face.

Lucas, Michael, and I walked into the dungeon. The place was trashed. There were spikes razor saw blades, poison darts, and sprung traps in the first one hundred feet. I kept my eyes peeled just in case there was another trap.

Michael walked us through to the labyrinth part with ease. He really did destroy the traps so the traps didn't trigger again. I saw a corridor that led to left and right. This was the beginning of the maze. It was mossy, damp, and had a weird sulfur smell.

I looked around the area and tried to use X-ray to see through some of the walls. The walls were thick, but I did get a gauge and saw the right side had a dead end. We went left. I was having a hard time seeing through the dark passages. Hunters usually have Flare, but I got mostly attack skills. I was hoping that I could get that skill soon.

The Scan skill lightened up the room and I was able to see everything, but the boys. They were tripping over their own two feet. No wonder Michael was having such a hard time. He was going crazy fast and probably ran into many walls in search of the end.

I could hear rats in the distance, but my Scan didn't pick them up yet. Rats can be small in this world, or they can be ten feet long. The ten-foot ones are the rats to worry about since their teeth are long enough to bite you in half.

One of the rats found us. His size was about six feet. I said, "Don't move there is a rat in front of us."

Michael lit the room up with his purple lightning and sliced up the rat hardcore style. Fur, guts, and blood got slashed into my face. I believe part of its stomach was in my hair just dangling. I promised myself I wouldn't scream. If I scream, it may alert the rest of the rats.

Michael yelled, "I see like a hundred of these things. Come take a look."

His loud voice woke the rats in the cave. Lucas stood in front of me. He recognized how stupid Michael was for doing that. I shot a bunch of arrows into the air and sparked them up with my Star Spark skill. The sparks lit up the cave a bit and Lucas could see, but barely.

Michael stepped back to us and smiled. He said, "Watch this."

The rats stormed in. I had my arrows head shot quite a few of them. Michael put on this Hell Armor and fought each of them with his swords. The blood spatter was so bad that Lucas just stood in front of me trying to take on all the guts and blood. He used his shield to deflect most of it but didn't get all of it.

Lucas really was a good big brother in his own way. Even if he was born after me. The rats were sneaking by and getting close to me. Lucas used his shield to beat them mercilessly. The echo from each bash caused a minor amount of debris to fall from the ceiling.

I used my arrows to penetrate the brains of each rat that came forward. The rat's bodies were stacking up and creating a fortified wall that smelled awful. Michael was nowhere to be found as he ran ahead to kill as many as possible.

After five minutes of fighting, the dungeon grew silent once again. The rats ran away. Something didn't feel right. That was way too easy. I wonder if Michael was their primary target since he couldn't be seen or dealt with.

Lucas dropped his shield down and got on one knee. He said, "That was a close one. Looks like we scared them off."

I said, "Get your ass back up. Get it up NOW!"

A sentient boulder found us and Lucas drove his shield right into it. The shield held it in place. The grunting was echoing through the cave. The rats abandoned us because they were afraid of the damn boulder.

I shot Fire Arrows into the boulder hoping it would slowly get destroyed without blowing up the dungeon. Each shot slowly chipped away at the boulder. The rock on the boulder's shell was getting chipping away and getting sharper. The edges were damaging Lucas's shield. His shield kept bending and breaking, but because of his healing magic. It kept repairing itself.

I tore through the boulder with my Flame Arrows enough that a small light in the center showed. I wasn't sure, but it appeared it was the boulder's core. I had to focus and make sure the Fire Arrow got inside and blew the thing up. I pulled back and charged the shot a bit. The shot was held for a few seconds and I let loose.

The Fire Arrow hit inside the boulder and blew up. I put too much of a charge on it and it caused a big explosion. Lucas saw that we were fucked and pulled me in close to him. He called out, "Barrier" and shielded the two of us.

The ceiling fell down on us and trapped us inside the dungeon. I didn't know what to say. That was my mistake. I charged the Flame Arrow a bit to much. I was worried that Lucas couldn't handle things. He had a disappointed look on his face. Lucas knew I was better than that. I was usually the calm and collected member of the group. But a that moment. I lost control

I heard outside the barrier a voice. It was Michael asking, "Are you in there?! Are you alright?!"

Michael was frantically digging through the collapse. I could hear him using his sword to bash at the rocks into pieces. After a few seconds, I heard an intense high-pitched pinging sound that echoed through the labyrinth. I was afraid the sound was going to cause another collapse.

Michael cut us out of the collapse and saw that Lucas holding me in the barrier bubble tightly. I think he was slightly jealous because there was a weird face that he made. He looked at Lucas and shook his head.

Michael said, "Get a room you two."

I said, "He is my brother. Get over yourself."

Michael replied, "Not biologically. You could go to town with him and have many children. The world wouldn't care since there is no biological reason not to."

I felt so gross. Not just by the statement that he made, but by the fact that he was a little right. I just saw him as my goofy little brother who needed guidance all the time. Especially, when it came to the affairs of the heart.

I walked out of the hole that Michael made and with my Scan managed to get through the labyrinth. The room at the end of the labyrinth was dark. I could barely see what was going on.

I noticed a torch to the left of us. My bow was pulled out and did a quick Fire Arrow to ignite the torch. The torch was bright and lit up the whole room This was one of those "OH SHIT" moments in my life.

There were two sets of steps going up to a door. Both of the stairs were made of stone and curved meeting each other at the top. The water on the steps made them very slippery and had a little bit of shine to them.

In between at the bottom of the steps, was a hundred-foot troll that looked like he hadn't eaten humans in a long time. I was thinking he was the one going outside and shitting in the field but didn't know how.

I tried to tip-toe slowly through the dungeon. Lucas was walking, but his gear was clanging badly. The noise was a lot less than last year, but he still made so much noise. I wanted to kill him, but it was my dad's fault. My father told him this was his size because it allowed for growing room.

Michael walked into the room, and yelled, "Wow, that's a big bitch!"

So much for stealth. The troll woke up and grabbed his ten-foot club with his right hand. He stood up and began to growl at us. The club I believe was just a tree he pulled out of the ground. Some of the leaves were still attached to the bottom of the club. The troll was wearing a bear for a loin cloth and some weaved tree branches as a thong.

The troll yelled through the dungeon and the rocks fell from the ceiling. I felt like we were screwed. The troll was stronger than a hundred of us so how were we to get out of this predicament.

I shot my arrows into the air. Diego and Sylvia went in for the charge, but they were so small that their teeth didn't do anything, but tickle his flesh. The arrows were imbued with sparks and shot at the troll. The troll's skin was so dense that it bounced right off.

Michael flew into the air and got right in the troll's face. He said, "I know what this rod is for."

I thought Michael was going to stab the troll in the eye with the metal rod that he bought. He turned on his purple lightning and disappeared. Michael wasn't much of a team player yet. In fact, most of the time I don't think he thought this was a team sport at all. Michael just wanted to show off to Lucas I believed. They were both tough and could take a lot. Michael just had to one-up his friend so he would brag about it later.

The troll took three steps forward and tripped going downward. Lucas held his shield high above his head. He had to take on the pressure of the troll's body. As Lucas had the shield there the pelvic region of the troll fell on him. I was a bit faster and dodged the fall, but Lucas was not so lucky.

The blow downward hit Lucas's shield and smashed the wooden frame that protected or just clothed the troll. The eyes on the troll looked like it was going to pop out of its head. I never had that type of experience, but it looked like the troll was hurting really bad.

Lucas was holding up the troll. If he had lost his strength for even a second. It would have been death by tea bagging. I heard both Lucas and the troll grunting hard. The veins in Lucas's neck appeared to be bulging out.

Michael yelled, "I got him."

With the troll bent over, Michael took that metal rod and shoved it up the troll's ass. The troll was fidgeting around and rolled off of Lucas. The rod was stuck in his...ewww. The sound of the rod and Michael were clanging against the ground. The echoes were causing the rocks to fall from the cave. Michael was holding on for dear life.

Michael pushed the rod in so far that it couldn't be seen anymore. He truly believed this was the answer to killing the troll. The look on the troll's face said otherwise as it looked like it wasn't in pain, but was enjoying himself. The troll was moaning a sense of ecstasy.

Lucas and I just looked at one another. We both didn't believe this was actually happening. Michael was staring at the troll with a "What the fuck" look on his face. I guess the was a reason there was shit all over the front of the dungeon. It also explains why the guy was easily able to retrieve the metal rods.

The troll rolled over onto its belly trying to pull the metal rod, but was purring like a baby walrus as he tried. Michael formed two executioner blades with his hand and rammed them into the back of the troll.

Michael held onto the blades and slowly slid down the troll's back. The troll was in pain and tried to pull him off. He kept reaching backward, but Michael kept swinging around making new punctures into the troll's back.

This was my chance. I formed a Fire Arrow and charged it good. I just had to be careful not to go too far and collapse the dungeon on us again. I shot the arrow and hit the troll. The explosion was enormous and pierced the inside of the trolls.

The Fire Arrow drilled inside the troll's chest and embedded itself. The explosion ripped the troll into tiny pieces and launched them across the entire dungeon. I was splattered with so much blood that I tasted metal in my found. My hair was pieces of its lungs and heart. Part of the troll's skin was dangling off my left shoulder like I was wearing a cape. I felt so gross.

I spit the blood out of my mouth the best I could. This time Lucas guarded himself with the shield and left me stranded. Michael was blown into the wall and looked a little cross-eyed as he was getting his bearings back. He shook his head and stood back up. That boy isn't right in the head.

Michael smiled at me and said, "We did it."

I'm not sure if you can honestly say that we did it, but it was a victory. I stood and walked toward the steps. The boys followed me. I was leading the pack up the stairs to the door. The door was large enough for the troll but was a little heavy for me to pull.

Michael took long steps and raced to the door. He opened the door and three baby trolls were behind. They were around our height but had one tooth and were giggling. I felt a little bad that we just killed their father. I thought to myself. "What have I done?"

Michael said, "I got this."

I thought I was going to see a nurturing, loving side to him just like the children in the first world. I believed he was going to play with them and try to change them to not hate humans and work by our side. They were just babies after all.

Nope, he took out his sword and decapitated every one of them in the blink of an eye. I was kind of disappointed. The whole time I was been here. I never saw a nurturing loving side like I always dreamed he would have. He was just doing his thing and killing anything that he felt deserved it.

The heads rolled onto the ground. The one head hit an oversized chair that was meant for the father. The bodies poured out blood and got between my toes. The smell was awful as the babies shit their pants when they died. I was bloodied, sticky, and smelly, I knew it would take forever to get all this flesh out of my hair. The problem was that I was getting used to it. I was feeling emotionally damaged at the prospect of getting used to this type of carnage.

Michael opened the next door and there was all the gold and treasures. There had to be millions in gold waiting for us. The troll was guarding his life savings for his children. There were relics, weapons, and gold as far as the eye could see. On the other side of the room was another door. Michael opened it up. Another set of steps designed for a troll was there.

Michael popped open the door at the top of the dungeon. It led us outside to the sun again. A bunch of demi-humans that worked for my father were standing outside. When they saw Michael open the hatch forty feet from the entrance. The demi-humans ran over and applauded us.

The easiest way to get into the dungeon was the back door. It would have led us right to the treasure. That was a humiliating moment to realize there was an easy way to get to the goal. I chose the hard way twice now. Once in the Void and the other here.

I saw them and asked if they could help us haul the treasure. My father thought ahead and had them bring a wagon to haul all the treasure. He designed this whole thing to give us a learning experience. We wiped out an entire village, killed trolls, rats, and got soaked in organs just so he could test us.

The demi-humans gathered all the treasure and put us in the back the cart. I was glad the adventure was over. My muscles cried out that it was time to go home. I really wanted a bath, but it took three days to get home. There weren't any attacks on us, just the distance was that far away. This is how the story ended. So if you hear me complain about how gross it is to fight with these guys. There is a good reason.

Chapter 4

Two days had passed and we were still stuck in this cage. The goblins came by and sexually assaulted Delilah three times a day. The breeding of these things was really fast. Each pregnant girl gave birth to eight goblins within a twenty-four-hour period of time. Delilah had given birth twice now. She was malnourished and overworked.

I was proud of her. She didn't give up on life. I would do my best to prop up her head and try not to be noticed. The sounds echoing in the chambers were like ghosts in pain. Delilah didn't lose hope yet, but her skin was turning pale and dehydrated. Her hands were clammy and looked prunes from all the water on the ground.

I was getting the feeling that the boys were going to fail me. I was using the cup Delilah was using to gain water from the ceiling and drank it. I tried to give her some of the water, but she refused. She only wanted the water the goblins gave her. There might have been something in the water, but I wasn't going to refuse her what she wanted.

On the third day, I was feeling my camouflage wearing off. The ground was slippery and affected my camouflage a bit. I looked at Diego. He had a disturbed look on his face. Diego was tired of seeing all the atrocities in this place. He was still a little boy in a way, but was a young adult in this world.

Diego said, "In fifteen minutes, three more goblins are going to come in here and rape her again. We need to get out. You are running low and I don't have much left in mana. I don't wish to have you get spotted. You will be sacrificed like these girls."

The goblins carried rusted knives, swords, and clubs. If I stole one of their rusted knives, I might be able to kill a bunch before I die. I wasn't going out without a fight. I stood in the corner and waited. Just like clockwork the goblins came down into the breeding ground and opened up the cages.

The first one walked over to get on top of her. I didn't hesitate. My right hand grabbed the knife on his left side. I swung around and placed the blade on his skinny little neck. It took me less than a second to slice open his neck from his chest to his right ear. Green blood was pouring out onto Delilah. She was in such a shocked state from the last three days that it didn't bother her in the least. Delilah was laughing in glee. Her mental state was damaged enough that the green blood was a nice change of color from the dark damp environment she was used to.

The other two goblins were waving their arms looking for me. My Camouflage was so good that the water wasn't even reacting to my movements.

The goblins were yelling at each other in a weird language. For the sake of the story, we will call it Goblinese. I couldn't understand their language, but understood their body language. The little assholes were afraid.

I raised the knife upward and stabbed the one closest to me through the head. The tip of the blade went under his chin and came out of his right eye socket. The eyeball was now protruding from it's face. The goblins was gargling on its own blood. I believed it was crying out for help.

When I pulled out the blade green blood got all over me. I was now able to be seen. The glow of the blood and the stench was enough that the goblins could sense where I was. The goblin in the cage with me pulled out his knife and lunged at me. I dodged the attack. My body swung around him like I was ballerina and stabbed him in the back. I pulled out the blade while twisting it. I wasn't through yet. My blade stabbed him in the back three more times killing him.

My first reaction was to grab his knife. I needed to soak this place in goblin blood if I was going to survive. I stood at the ready all of the goblins to attack. This was going to be my moment of truth.

The girls were moaning and the goblins were being alerted. I felt a sense of betrayal as they all in unison said I was there. My fear was taking over, but didn't let it get to me.

There had to be a hundred goblins coming to my cage. The steps coming toward me were in unison. The pounding on the stone floor echoes throughout the cavern. I was really feeling fucked at that moment.

Diego said, "Burn this bitch to the ground. I got your back."

Even though the girls lured the goblins to my location. I still felt a sense of protecting the young girls in the place. I rattled the cage to get the attention of the horde. This was my do or die moment. I had to make it count.

The goblins ran to the entrance of my cage. A goblin stormed in foaming at the mouth like it had rabbis. I took the blades and stabbed a stabbed him in the chest. I took my left foot and kicked him backwards into the group. The blades were covered in green blood and flesh. The blades were dull enough that it was hard to pull them out of a goblins body.

The goblins were funneling into the cage. I was able to keep them under control for a moment, but that was just a moment as they pushed through into the cage and knocked me on my ass.

I smiled at them and used Instant Teleportation. I told you I learned a few moves throughout the years. I was getting on the goblin's shoulders one by one slicing their necks open. I used it repeatedly until I killed nineteen of the goblins.

I got myself to the front entrance. It looked like there were more goblins than before. I would say there was a thousand of them in the halls gathered up. Each goblin was foaming at the mouth ready to kill or rape me. I wasn't sure how this was going to go down.

I did have an escape plan in place. I was going to use X-ray to see outside as I was hoping to teleport through the door. The problem is that I wasn't experienced enough to know get through to other side without getting stuck in the door. This would have been a big gamble on my part that end with my cutting my body in half. I could feel in in my bones. The end of this day was not going to go well for me.

I was prepared to fight for my life. I called out a warrior's call as I raised the right knife into the air. The goblins looked at me strangely. I could see fear in their eyes for the first time since the fight began.

The room was quiet for a moment. I heard a hard knock on the door behind me. The door had a large wooden bar lock. It would take ten goblins to get it off because of the thick and large the beam was. I wasn't able to get it off to get outside, but whatever was on the outside sounded strong and fierce. I thought well there goes my escape.

I heard a voices coming from the door. My boys finally came to get me. I recognized Michaels's voice anywhere. His voice was very distinct as he was hitting puberty and had a weird manliness and a child sound to it. It often squeaked, but I always found it cute.

Michael said, "Why do you even bother with a shield? It's a blunt object that you don't have the right strength to manage. I think you should just use your Executioner Blade. You have no defense. Every time someone hits you your body opens up and takes the piercings. Lucas was a real tank that could actually take a hit."

Paine exclaimed, "Fuck you! I take hits all the time and guess who is still alive!"

Paine continued to hit the door with the shield. The goblins were staying back. I think they felt something coming from the door and appeared to be afraid.

The goblins were afraid of the groups aura. Between Michael and Paine, I was nothing to them. There was also the possibility that with their hive mind. The goblins managed to see what happened to the guards outside. If I know my boys, there are goblin corpses everywhere outside.

Paine gave up and put his shield into the void storage. He swung the large sword down breaking in the door. Each hit came downward slicing into the door. A small hole was formed right at the lock bar.

Paine said, "Here is the problem. That's a thick ass lock bar."

Pain put his arm inside. He put his right hand underneath and tossed it to the left of him. The bar went flying and broke a cage that had a young thirteen-hour pregnant girl inside. Paine flew open the doors and smiled.

Michael said, "The cavalry is here. He saw the women and bad shape. I was standing there by the door. My clothes were dirty and wet. I looked malnourished like the rest of the girls. I saw a seething hatred in his eyes. I had a few scratches from being attacked.

Michael didn't bother to ask what was going on. He drew purple lightning and charged straight into the horde of goblins. In the blink of an eye, the goblins were all dead. He decapitated all of them. The bodies were slowly falling to the ground and spraying green blood everywhere.

Loraine ran over and opened the cages to get the girls out of them. She didn't need a key. Loraine just used a smite on each lock to get them out. Paine was slower so he used his Void Spheres on the locks to get them open. The girls were looking relieved to get out, but some of them were so psychologically damaged that they didn't wish to leave.

I walked up the steps at the end of the hall. I was checking on the other floors because the cages went up three floors. We had to rescue all the girls in the breeding chambers. You take away their reproduction source. They will all die off of old age.

I went up the steps and Michael had the floors filled with dead goblins. I was walking through trying to dodge all the blood on the floor. The one goblin had a pair of keys. I took them and began opening up the cages. There were so many girls in here that I couldn't imagine where they got them all.

Each girl really needed clothes and a bath. They smelled horrible and looked even worse. The girls had so many scars on their bodies that I don't think a single man would ever want to touch them. It might actually have been for the better, because if these things happened to me. I would never want a man to touch me.

I should have been paying better attention. Michael missed three goblins while I was opening a cage. The goblins pulled me off the cage and dragged me up the stairs. My butt was bouncing up the stairs as two of them had me by the arms and one had me by the hair.

I was trying to catch my balance as I was brought up two flights of stairs. Once I got to the top there was an altar with candles in a circle around it. There was a painting of what looked to be some kind of demon above it.

The demon had a black cloak, no shirt, and black leather pants. The demon's hair was purple and long. The ears were pointed and had vicious fangs coming out of its mouth.

The demon appeared to be surrounded by many trees with eyes on them. The bark was shaped like teeth with blood running down them. Some of the trees looked white, black, and brown.

The photo had a pregnant elf bowing to the demon. The ears were pointed and long. There was a weird look of sadness as she was surrounded by eight tiny creatures. It looked like she was asking for something.

The goblin that had me by the hair took out his knife and placed it against my throat. I couldn't move as he nicked my throat a bit. A little bit of blood went down my neck. The goblin stuck out his long tongue and licked it up. The tongue had to have been nine inches long. I thought to myself. Where were the men like this back in the first world?

Michael made it to the top of the steps and saw I was a hostage. I could see the fury in his eyes. He was hesitant since he could accidentally cut my head off in the process. His eyes were pure purple with intensity.

The room was enormous as an aisle was open in the center and each side had over a thousand goblins. Each goblin was wearing red robes and a black sash. It appeared to be some kind of goblin cult. The ground was made of stones with a large red carpet leading to the altar.

The goblins were raising their hands into the air praying to something. The shadows from the six torches in the rooming made them look a lot more intimidating than they are.

I was being dragged to the altar slowly. Some of my hair was falling out of my head. I was afraid he was going to pull out an entire patch of it. Last thing I needed was to look like I was going bald.

Michael was waiting for him momentarily. He didn't need to worry about me for one second. I used Instant Teleportation and wrapped my legs around the neck of the goblin holding a knife on me. I spun around and flipped him backward with my legs. The movement was so violent that I broke his neck in the process.

Diego and Sylvia brought the hyenas into the room. I could sense their bloodlust. Diego shared memories with Sylvia as part of their guardian bond. After what they witnessed the goblins do to the girls. Both of them wanted payback. I saw my spirits merge with the hyenas. Their mouths were drooling and aggressively barking. They were about to kill the room.

I picked up the goblin's knife and charged at the one that held my left arm. The knife was jabbed into his chest three times and curved the blade in to slice open its throat. The blood had a putrid smell like garbage.

The last goblin that brought me up the stairs was looking at me. I lunged at him and pinned him to the ground. He tried to push me off. I had the blade going downward toward his right eye. The goblin wasn't strong and it slowing went into it's eye. Blood and puss were coming out of it as the goblin squirmed in agony.

I pinned down goblin's left arm because it was trying to protect its face. The knife went into the left socket allowing me to shovel out that eye. I was gaining a great sense of satisfaction from torturing these animals. I loved hearing him scream in pain and agony.

I opened the goblins mouth and shoved the knife up into its brain from the roof of its mouth. It was a high-pitched squeal that ended when he lost his breath. This was how you kill these evil bitches.

Sylvia and Diego used Predator and ran into the right side of the room. The goblins were crying out in pain as they tried to stab my beautiful animals. The hyena's skins were so strong that the knives couldn't penetrate them.

I could sense their bloodlust like my own. The hyenas were ripping out their through with their death. Some of them were even eaten alive. Their fragile weapons were nothing compares to the claws and teeth of my beautiful babies.

Michael shot lightning everywhere. He wanted vengeance for all the things these evil beasts did to these girls. He disappeared and the heads on the left side were flying into the air. Splattering blood all over the place.

The sweet screams of the goblins became music to my ears. It was like a symphony of terror to an entire race of evil. There is nothing more gratify than prey out of predators.

There were candles around the altar that were a nice glow to them. A glow that needed to be enlightened for the sake of the girls. This place needed to be burned to the ground. I took the lit candles surrounding the altar to the demon. This was going to only end one way. I set the candles directly under the portrait of the demon and the elf. This place was the driest spot in the cave. The bottom refused to burn at first, but it got there eventually. The burning filled smoke throughout the room and it was becoming increasingly hard to see.

A small flame hit the body of a goblin. The blood was bein set on fire. It appeared that goblin blood was a flammable source. This was good to know. I do have Flame Arrows after all.

Michael ran over to me and looked into my eyes. After killing all his goblins. I was feeling a little weak and nervous. What was going on with him? Michael was looking at me really intensely. The flames surrounding us was making me feel hotter than I already was.

Michael went in for the kiss and held there for a long time. I couldn't fight it. This was the moment I waited for for a long time. He missed me and was choosing me at that very moment. The heat was making my sweat before we even got to do anything.

Michael grabbed my ears and pulled me in even closer. I had no idea until that moment, but right behind my ears really made me horny. I wanted him to fuck me right there in the room on fire. I didn't care if there were dead bodies everywhere. There seem to always be dead bodies everywhere when hanging out with him.

I jumped up and altar with my legs spread open waiting for him to take me. He turned around and said, "Okay, let's go Diego and Sylvia killed their last goblin and we need to get out of here. The place is on fire."

Why did I have to set that stupid thing on fire? I felt the urge and he is the one being rational right now. I got off the altar and jumped on Diego. Diego ran down the steps and out the front door. The area was filled with over five hundred girls.

Some of the girls were insane and tried to run back into the burning chambers. There was a weird aura around them that seemed to find comfort in the goblins way of life. I wasn't sure what cause their minds to flip like a switch, but they didn't want to be alive if they were getting inseminated by the vile beasts. Their brains had a hard time telling what was reality.

The baby goblins were never found, but I'm sure they were in the building. The fire was going to burn them alive. I could smell the stench of goblin flesh burning throughout the chambers. Their blood was acting like fuel to the flames. The smoke was green and flowing throughout the chambers. It was a sickly smell that made you want to vomit, and some of the girls actually did.

The girls were the first to leave the chambers. I watched them all to make sure that nobody got burned alive. Michael had to physically carry out many of them because they were too stubborn to leave or too weak.

I followed girls out and watched as the large doors were burning. The chambers were filled with mist and smoke that blended. You could see the smoke coming out of several holes in the side of the cavern that once was. The destruction of the building was gratifying to say the least.

The sky was filled with dark clouds. It looked like it was about to rain and hard. I knew that could only be one thing. Matilda stayed outside to hunt down people who were escaping. She knows how to manipulate the weather and strike things down dead.

Matilda would always start with a little ice. She made sure their bodies were perfectly still so she could cackle while striking them down easily. The madness in her eyes was strange as they turned white with lightning surrounding them.

Matilda would float across the land like a god to intimidate. She was realized early on how to fly using wind magic. Matilda would destroy her enemies was great distances and rarely ran out of magic. People in the kingdom often were afraid of her that were weak. Her biggest flaw was that she was physically weak and easily killed so this was her best way to evade predators.

The goblin's body parts were blown to pieces throughout the sands. The lightning was sharp and crystalizing the sands. Matilda wouldn't let a single goblin escape. I would like to say that she did it to save those girls, but she just loved to kill people and things. She just kept getting stronger from it and faster with her spells.

No water was falling from the sky to put out the fire so everything connected to the chamber went up in smoke. Just what we needed more heat in a desert. The smoke was high and I believed after a while the goblins would notice that we torched the place.

Paine said, "We need to go."

Matilda replied, "But there are more of them. I want to kill them all."

Paine responded, "You will get your chance. What we just did here today was a declaration of war. The goblins are going to want revenge."

Matilda scoffed at him but did what he asked. She didn't wish to be left behind. There was no carriage or horses so I'm not sure what was going on with that. They must have lost them in the storm.

The girls walked through the desert in hopes of getting to Zahn. Pain believed he knew the way, but wasn't sure. His stops and a crazy amount of food helped us with our journey. The man was a prepper for sure.

I had never seen so much food in my life and it was fresh. I'm talking food right off an apple tree fresh. The steak was off limits though from the tavern. Michael was trying to eat some just to piss off Paine. The truth was he found the apple stash and never wanted to leave. I think he ate sixty apples in one sitting. I knew he liked apples, but that was excessive.

The journey was really tiring. The girls wanted Paine to just carry them in the Void Storage, but he refused since the whole time thing was a problem. We really could have used a Portal Master Creationist to help haul all these winey ass girls to the city.

The group came across a small village in the middle of nowhere. Rest seemed to be the best course of action. Maybe they had a bunch of water. Michael was being weird about his water supply. I believe the gargoyles were running low and having over five hundred girls in total need water was depleting his resources.

Matilda was getting sick of listening to them fight through the desert and kept begging for us to kill them off. Some of the girls were trying to help the mentally ill in the group. The heat wasn't helping them at all.

Once we got to the village, the place was filled with scared folks. The village had fewer people than girls we brought with us. I knew that they wouldn't be able to truly help us, but maybe we could buy supplies from them.

Paine stood at the front of the group. A man came out. He had to be sixty years old. His legs were shaking and half his hair was missing. I would say every other hair was gone and thinned out. The old man had a cloak made of wyrm skin to help protect him from the sun.

The man asked, "Can I help you folks?"

I replied, "A few of us are adventurers on a journey to Zahn. These ladies behind us were trapped by the goblins and we freed them. We mean no trouble. I was just hoping for water, some shade, and directions to Zahn."

The man responded, "I can give you some of those things, but for the water, we are in short supply ourselves. If you freed these girls, then you are talking about the breeding grounds. I would say that you must be strong to take on that many goblins. But you may have just killed everyone in Zahn. They don't have the strength to take one eighteen million goblin forces."

I said, "Then we will help them fight to our dying breath."

The man replied, "You are to leave this town immediately. You go south for about six miles in that direction. Do not stop for anything. Get these girls safe to their families and loved ones."

The journey was rough, but listened to him. We already walked twenty miles. Six miles in the right direction didn't seem so bad. The journey continued and the girls were exhausted. I can see why though. They spent most of their days on their back just taking it for a while. There wasn't a whole lot of room for exercising or even wanting to be alive for that matter.

Once we got to the two-mile marker. The girls began to act like savages. I think they were losing hope that we were to find the place. There was no sign of life or that we were even getting close to the city. The girls were getting into fistfights. The agitation of these girls was bad. I shouldn't have expected better considering they are mostly my age and psychologically damaged. The heat was boiling their brains.

Michael ran in there and broke up quite a few fights. The girls were completely naked so their skin was boiling from the sun. The only thing that Michael was able to do was to pop rocks out of his mouth and tell the girls to stick them under their tongues. I had no idea why the girls were fighting over the rocks. Some of the girls would tell him that they would fuck him for another rock.

I just toughed it out walking through the desert. Eating a regurgitated rock didn't seem that good to me. I think I'll tough this one out. The rocks had water in them when the girls were thirsty. The water in the rocks replenished them. I kind of feel bad for Michael. He will have to put all those girls' saliva back into him. EEEWWW!

The walking continued for many miles. The sun was burning our flesh and the girls' feet were burnt to a crisp. The bottoms were raw and the blisters were harsh. I wanted something that would cover me better, but my clothes were all I had.

The city of Zahn was in our sight and the guards were looking very closely as they saw a herd of young naked girls walking toward the gates. The gates were closed because not many people traveled the desert to reach them. Most of the crops were made within the city walls and covered the Northeast part of the city.

With the help of Water and Earth Mages, they are able to grow anything they wanted in the desert. I was actually stunned to see how much it flourished. The city was more stone and had hardened mud on the outside of the buildings. Because of the bad weather, they often had to repair the buildings.

The gates were drawn down and one of the guards recognized the girl he loved growing up. The guard knew that these were the missing girls. He lifted his visor and opened his arms for the girl. That was the happiest I saw of any of the girls the whole time I was around them. She kissed the guard and people came to flock around the girls.

One by one people were coming to see if their family members had returned to them. This was a glorious moment for the families in the city of Zahn. People were in tears of joy as they were reunited with their loved ones.

A man who looked to be blind was with a priestess. He walked over to Paine and grabbed his hand. They pulled into each other and slammed shoulders hard enough it almost knocked people around them off their feet.

The man said, "Good to see you brother."

That had to be just a phrase. The man was clearly blind. The only thing that had me curious was how did he know Paine. They seemed to have a cozy relationship together. Another sign that he might be gay.

Paine looked at us and said, "This is David. We ran a dungeon together once. He was one of five survivors if I remember correctly. The beautiful woman by his side is Angela. She was named after the angel, and turns out is guided by her too. Strange world."

Angela put out her hand and said, "Pleasure to meet you."

This was the beginning of a political war.

Chapter 5

Angela let go of my hand. She had a smile on her face because the saving of these girls was a true victory. The king had orders that claimed anyone who went against the goblin treaty would be executed. Whenever a girl was kidnapped the people had to look the other way.

The goblins outnumbered the people of Zahn eighteen to one. Most of the people in the city weren't trained to kill goblins or anything for that matter. There were normal people who cooked, cleaned, farmed for the kingdom, and did trades. The number of guilds were half that of Tryanon. If they went to war with the goblin, you would be expecting farmers to defend the city because heroes were in short supply.

A guard walked over to us and asked, "Who is in charge here?"

Paine immediately raised his hand. I don't think any of us were really in charge, but the man was immortal. If the punishment for his crime was execution, he was the best suited for it. Paine clearly thought this through as he came to save me.

The guard said, "Come with me."

Paine smiled as he walked behind the guard. We all followed him to act as representatives. David and Loraine also followed them to the castle. The city was huge and felt like it took forever to walk there.

Once we got to the castle, a group of guards asked us to drop our weapons at the gate. Paine even dropped his armor. He wanted to do his best to appear defenseless. The truth was he just used the armor to store magic power and mana.

The guards had spears pointed at us. I don't think they wanted any trouble, but the word was that we started a war with the goblins. To be fair, the word was true. I'm proud of what we did.

We walked up a stairwell. The stones reminded me of the ones in Tryanon. In fact, the castle design was almost exactly the same. It was like the original architects were the same people. They did say that the people made the cities around the holy sites. I just never thought it was the same people designing them.

The group reached the top. Matilda was lagging behind since her class was mental and not physical. I was having a hard time myself. Hunters were supposed to be agile and fast. I just have a hard time doing things like this over long distances.

I learned a new trick from the animals that I spoke to in the cage. Apparently, I can shrink my hyenas to the palm of my hand. I had them sitting in my right breast pocket. This was a new concept that required my spirits to be inside the hyenas the whole time. I called them Pocket Puppies. It was a connection to my Predator ability so I didn't need to be blessed to use it.

There were wooden doors that weren't open. I was just hoping that I wouldn't see another fat fuck banging a young girl again. That was one of the grossest things I ever saw. I feel like I'm going to vomit just thinking about it.

The doors were opened and a man in his late twenties was on the throne. He was muscular and skinny. He had a crown that barely fit the top of his head. The king had no shirt on and washboard abs. I went from I hope not to see a naked fat guy to do me instantly.

The king was over seven feet tall and his sides were squished in the chair. I would say he was a powerful Barbarian. Barbarians tend to be more savage than anything. The fact that the issue wasn't resolved already in a warlike manner was puzzling.

The group walked in and bowed to the king except Paine. He had a weird thing about bowing to no man. This would often piss off every king we ever came across, but respect between the two parties was often earned anyway.

The king said, "I am Augustus Grunon. The king of Zahn. I see you aren't bowing. Why?"

Paine said, "I bow to no man. Especially one that is weaker than myself. If you catch me bowing to you. Know this. I am plotting your demise."

Augustus looked at him puzzled and smiled. He said, "Kill him."

The guard ran over and rammed their spears into his chest. They pierced right through his chest and made it out his back. The ends of the spears resembled that of an arrowhead. The sides curved back. The design was to pierce the skin and hook the victim on the way back.

Paine said calmly, "Was that necessary? You tore my shirt."

Augustus was in shock. The man didn't just take spears to the chest but showed no signs of being hurt by them. This was truly queer in his eyes. He walked over and evaluated to see if the spears went through. Being that close to Paine was truly dangerous. I wasn't sure if he was going to Void Sphere his head off.

Augustus said, "Take out the spears."

The men yanked on the spears driving the sharp edges into Paine's flesh. The damage of tearing his shirt was getting to him more than the actual gouging of his flesh. The guards were clearly weak and couldn't seem to pull the spears out of his chest.

Paine asked, "Why aren't you pulling from the other direction. This direction is just destroying my shirt and pissing me off."

The guard looked back at Augustus and he nodded to do what he said. The end of the spear had another piece that would get stuck. So Paine grabbed the spears and snapped them all in half to make it easier to pull out. The guards pulled the spears out and dropped the blood-stained pieces on the floor.

Augustus asked, "What kind of warrior are you?"

Paine replied, "I am a simple paladin. Still trying to figure out what kind of paladin as my shield does nothing for me. My team believes that I am a Retribution Paladin that heals really fast."

Augustus asked, "Do you know what crime you have committed?"

Paine said, "I have committed no crimes at all. The goblins kidnapped my comrade and I went to her aid. In the process, we were ambushed. My team killed them all in self-defense. The girls would have died of starvation if I hadn't saved them. So we freed your people."

Augustus replied, "Freed my people. You have just damned them all. Their numbers outweigh ours eighteen to one. You just damned everyone in the kingdom. The goblins show no mercy and will kill every person here and rape every woman. The few do not outweigh the many."

Paine said, "For a Barbarian, you are truly a coward, aren't you. You let them rape your women so that you don't have to defend them. Who exactly are you defending? Was it a coward who made the law to instill fear in its own people?"

Augustus rebutted, "It was my great great grandfather who made the treaty with the goblins. Our numbers have grown and wouldn't exist without that treaty. My soldiers are strong, but don't have the strength to defend against that many."

Paine challenged his resolve, "What if we fight with you?" We took out over three thousand of them and didn't even break a sweat."

Augustus said, "Or maybe I give you up to the goblins and see if we can keep the treaty as is."

I said, "That won't work."

Augustus replied, "She speaks. The hunter woman speaks. What would a half-wit who got captured in the first place be able to do? Before you ask, how I know it was you, you reek of the breeding chambers. How many children did you birth while in there."

Michael put his head down. He didn't want to think about the horrible things that happened to me. Michael was just glad that I was alive and felt horrible for not being there when I needed him the most.

I said, "Zero."

Augustus was shocked. He wasn't sure if I was telling the truth. So he challenged me. The guy liked to challenge people. This was clearly a trait of the Barbarians. I could see him fidgeting with his hands. He was looking for some sort of action. I think he was getting aroused by our conversation.

Augustus asked, "How did you accomplish this this? Did you fight for many straight days?"

I said, "There is far more to a fight than simply swinging an axe or shooting a bow. I hid in the darkness waiting for the perfect opportunity to strike."

Augustus looked disappointed. He was hoping to hear the tale of how I fought off thousands of goblins over the course of my stay. He had no idea what to expect, but I let him know one thing. I was a tactician and not a savage.

Augustus asked, "So why do you believe that I can't restore the treaty?"

I said, "Because you would be at war with the nation of Tryanon."

Augustus was intrigued. He had no idea who we really were. His eyes lit up and wanted to hear us out. He walked over and sat back down in his throne chair. The chair looked like it was about to break under his weight.

Augustus asked, "Why would I be at war with Tryanon?"

I said, "Matilda and I are the princesses of Tryanon. King Draco Simpson now sits on the throne. We are one of eight Simpson sisters."

The turn of events just changed. I saw the worry in his eyes. That would mean we weren't just heroes, but diplomats from the kingdom of Tryanon. The situation was a no-win for him. He could keep the treaty, but lose the kingdom to Tryanon. Tryanon was the paladin capital of the world. He would battle us or be taken over by the goblins. Either way he had a fight on his hand. Things didn't look good for his people.

Augustus thought he would have the upper hand in this situation and the tables turned so fast. He was breathing heavily and going through every scenario in his head. Augustus had only one choice. He needed to ask for Tryanon's aid.

Augustus said, "You put me into quite the predicament. If you are truly royalty, then may I ask for your aid. I need enough troops to take down the goblin army."

I replied, "You have all the aid you need in this room."

Augustus was almost in tears. How could only five people from the kingdom of Tryanon possibly defeat that many goblins? Michael powered up and put on his Hell Armor. He was going to show what he was made of.

Augustus replied, "So you have a demon with you. A man who appears to be immortal. A Priestess that seems somehow connected to the immortal. A sister who looks like some sort of mage. And of course, there is you the kidnapped girl that has no place in a true battle because she can't take care of herself. Did I get that right?"

Augustus was infuriating. I was tossed through a sandstorm. My defenses aren't the same as his. This guy spoke too much. I couldn't figure out if he was testing us. He got off his throne and got within an inch of my face. I didn't flinch one bit. Augustus took his right hand and placed it on my chin. He gave me a kiss on my right cheek. The kiss sent shivers down my spine.

I couldn't see Michael's face, but his body language said he wanted to kill the king. When the king wasn't looking he flicked him off. I never saw him get jealous before. The purple in his armor was dimming as if it were connected to his emotions. I would think anger would make them brighter. I looked more like despair.

Augustus walked over to David. He saw that he was somehow involved in all of this. He seemed to know David well. There was no way I was going to tell him that we were sent on a quest to pick a fight with the goblins.

David said, "Greetings king."

Augustus just scowled at him. He said, "So what was your involvement in all of this."

David asked, "Why do you plan to give me to goblins?"

Augustus replied, "Don't tempt me, brother."

Paine said, "Wait you two are brothers. You look nothing alike."

David said, "There are three of us. Augustus, David, and Solomon. Solomon is the youngest. Our father had three mistresses. So same dad, different moms. Our moms were treated well until they got sick and died alongside our father."

Augustus added, "I became king because I'm the oldest."

David replied, "It was by three months and it was too hard with me being blind."

Augustus smiled and asked, "What, can a man not work in the dark?"

David said, "Fuck you."

Augustus and David both laughed. The room was beginning to ease up. People didn't realize that the king's brother sent the mission. Well, we didn't know, but Malcolm probably did. That man is a crafty snake.

David said, "You are really getting smooth as you get older. Maybe a woman would actually want to be with you."

Augustus replied, "Not once have I forced a woman to be in my company. Just because you're a one-woman man. Does not mean I have to be."

Augustus said, "There is no way around this. Get yourselves ready. You started this mess and now you will clean it up."

David stayed behind with Angela. I wasn't sure what we got ourselves into. How is this man going to expect the five of us to kill eighteen million goblins? I closed my eyes and couldn't think of anything. Michaels is fast, but can't take out that many. There seems to be an adrenaline-timer to his Overdrive. Overdrive is still a passive skill, but he has to get his heart rate to a certain point for it to work.

I had to think of a strategy. I was walking down the stairs slowly. My eyes never left the steps as we were walking. I couldn't see any future where we could win. The only thing we had that the goblins didn't was the walls. The walls would be nothing though if they had wyverns

Wyverns were dragon-like creatures. They were smaller so goblins could ride on their backs. Their tongues could get up to fifteen feet and had a twenty-foot wingspan. Their teeth were sharp and had enough pressure to penetrate my hyena's skin. The tail had six large bones that curved upward. The tail was often used as a weapon. Wyvern, like dogs, were very loyal to a master that fed them. The downside was that if you didn't feed them. You were the meal.

Paine saw me aggravating over the situation. He held my right shoulder and said, "I got this don't worry. The first stop we have is to a weaponsmith. Sometimes they have a good Creationist."

I thought a weapon upgrade would be the perfect place to start. I could feel my bow giving way under the weight of my power when I got attacked by the wyrm. I'm glad they found the bow. I wondered how much time they spent trying to find it.

The group got to the gate. Paine opened a portal and put all our weapons and gear we didn't need inside. He set it in an area close to this bedroom setup. Paine was collecting a lot of weapons, clothes, and armor for every situation. I kind of envied him for having an endless closet of clothes.

The market was busy so we went to a tavern. The group sat down and grabbed some ale. With the size of most of us, nobody would have guessed we were only fifteen in this world. The age was usually eighteen to drink. Strange world when you are expected to marry at fourteen but drink at eighteen. How the hell are we supposed to deal with the men in our lives?

I sat down and ordered a salad. I was trying to lay off the meat. After the event with the boys at the dungeon, I would only eat meat from home. I knew it was taken care of and safe. Paine looked at me. He had a smile on his face.

Paine said, "The meat is good. Why are you eating like a rabbit?"

Michael would always say the exact same thing to me. What is wrong with being a rabbit? They are kind creatures that I used to hold when I was a child. I was getting all the proteins I needed from the vegetables.

Michael came in with a bag of apples he bought and sat down. Michael said, "Can I get an ale here."

Michael had taken his armor off. He didn't want to scare the townspeople. He wore that skin-tight black shirt and black shorts that enhanced his manhood. I tried not to look, but it was hard not to notice. The other girls would look and it would piss me off. I wasn't sure if he did it for attention, but all the ladies noticed and smiled. I loved him, but he wasn't thinking about stuff like this. I couldn't believe I had to fight for his attention around every corner.

I ate my salad and drank one ale. I didn't want to get hammered, but felt a little tipsy after one. From that point forward, I drank water. The water was nice since the owner was a Water Mage who did ice magic. Every morning the woman would form a large ice block and tangle it from the ceiling. The ice would melt into the cup to stay cool for the day as the temperatures rose. I drank her water as if it was going out of style.

Michael was eating his apples and staring at the table. There was a knot in the wooden table that he kept playing with. Michael swigged his pint and followed the designs with his left hand. There was something about it that mesmerized him. He wasn't paying attention to the group at all.

I walked over to Michael and said, "Are you okay?"

Michael replied, "We need more firepower. I am so used to doing things alone that I finally hit a point where I need you guys. Every time we went on adventures I would do everything in my power to protect you and Lucas. I hit a point now where I'm just trying to protect you and Matilda. I can't fail like I failed Lucas."

I said, "You can't fail me because I can take care of myself. I was alone for days without you and came out okay. I had faith that you would come and save the day. I wasn't wrong you came in with fire in your heart and killed most of them. Just don't go soft on me.

Michael picked up an apple and bit into it. The juice was running down his chin. He had that boyish charm still. The fact that he is part demon seems foreign to me. I don't know why everyone is afraid of him. Michael has been and always will be a kind soul that protects the people he loves.

Paine asked the waitress where we could get some good weapons. The woman replied, "You might be able to get some from the Martin's shop. It's about six buildings down and take a right. You see the sign that has a piece of meat on it you go down six houses and take a left. He will be the sixth building on the right. Did you get all that?"

Paine said, "I got it. Thanks for the advice. We will go check it out."

Paine stood up and finished off his ale. Paine said, "Let's go family we got some serious work to do. I don't know how long it will take for the goblins to get here."

The group got up and we walked out. Paine gave the woman a very generous tip. He had enough gold that it would take millions of years to use it all. He really made good as he went from a boy in the slums to one of the richest men in the world and that was only because he was a dungeon survivor.

The group made it to the weapon's shop. A black man standing over an anvil pounding away at steel. The man's clothes were a white cotton shirt with holes in it and a pair of black trousers. The dirt on the man was thick and looked like peasant clothing. The place was hot and the man was very sweaty. As he sweats, it looks like it disappeared into the darkness of his skin.

A white man came out and asked, "Can I help you? Names Martin"

Michael said, "We are looking for powerful weapons that will help slaughter the goblins if they show."

Martin said, "I have plenty of wares ranging from twenty to sixty gold. They are made of the finest metals."

Paine was staring at the black man. He noticed the collar on him. The black man was a slave hero who worked in this shop. Paine was watching the man craft as Martin was blabbering on about his wares.

The black man began to take off his shirt. His back was covered in pink scars. The pain from those scares must have been excruciating. A bunch of the scars looked fresh as if he either never healed or were made that morning.

Paine asked, "Your wares are fine, but I'm looking at your slave."

Martin said, "He's not for sale."

Paine countered, "I will give you one thousand gold for him."

Paine was looking for an armory and got a better idea. He wanted an army more.

Chapter 6

Martin's eyes lit up like a Christmas tree. The cost of keeping up with slaves and the materials. Martin was probably making two gold a sword. With the amount of money Paine was offering him, he could easily buy ten in his place.

Martin said, "Make it two thousand gold."

Martin was clearly greedy and didn't care for the black man at all. He was whipping and abusing him. Who knows what he actually did to him? Paine had enough money for a million slaves at this price.

Michael said, "It's wrong to buy a human being, Paine."

Paine rebutted, "Don't you have like a thousand slaves."

Michael said, "They aren't just slaves. They are family. Just because you have a disposable income doesn't mean you should use it to give us canon fodder."

Paine said, "Two thousand it is. Let's head down to the slave center in your town and get him transferred to me."

Martin said, "Stop what your doing. Looks like you're getting a new owner today. Don't know what he wants with you, but frankly, I don't care. You could just end up being his fuckboy. He does have that twinkle in his eye."

Paine looked at Martin disgusted. The man was a true pig. It was really hard to look at him, but he was leading the way. All of us got out of the shop and he turned around and locked the door.

Martin said, "Before we go there can I see the two thousand gold you are going to pay me."

Paine opened his portal to his Void Storage. He pointed at the gold Martin would receive. The more this man spoke. The angrier Paine was getting. Michael had a look on his face as he showed him the gold. He recognized something about the gold. I wondered if it was stolen by his face.

Paine said, "I will make a better deal for you. You can go in there and grab as much gold as you can get. I will let you have the biggest bag in the world as long as you can carry it."

Martin said, "Is that a challenge?"

Paine replied, "It's more of a game of chance. I don't believe you can get a lot of my gold."

Martin grabbed what looked like to be a giant backpack that would fill tens of thousands of gold pieces. What the hell was Paine thinking? He was rewarding this man's greed. There had to be a catch. From the stories I heard about him, he isn't just a masochist. He is a Sadist. On the journey through the forest, Paine bragged about holding over two hundred men in his storage for so long that they cannibalized each other. Even got the man to eat his own body. Is that what he is planning with this guy.

The group got to the slave trade area. I really wanted some water. The drinks at the tavern weren't enough. I really thought it would be. The trade area was hotter inside than it was outside. The trader was there asking for his two gold fee for the trade and collars.

Paine gladly paid the man for the cost. The collars alone cost a hundred silver to make. Paine was looking into the eyes of the black slave. His eyes had some red to them from exhaustion. There was black circles around the eyes and slouch in his back.

Martin said, "Release." and the collar came undone.

The trader put the new collar on and pricked Paine's finger. There was a small dot on the back of the collar. The collar lit up and the black man was now Paine's slave. We weren't sure what he wanted with a Creationist. In battle, they only repair gear and open a portals to weird utility places. Most Creationist talents don't come even close to Wong. Wong is a Portal Master and this guy seems to be a Craft Master. Without ideas or blueprints, this guy is worthless to us.

Paine said, "What is your name?"

The black man stared into his eyes like he was going to kill him. There was an intensity that made me believe Paine knew something that we didn't. The black man smiled. He was just playing nice for the moment but didn't know why he was bought to begin with.

The black man said, "Names Darwin."

Martin began to clear his throat. He was done messing around and wanted to get his gold and leave. Paine opened the portal and let the man inside. There appeared to be no funny business. He just wanted the guy that badly.

Martin ran in and started to laugh. He had never seen that much gold in his whole life. He knelt down and shuffled the gold into his bag. Paine turned Darwin around and had him look into the portal.

Martin yelled, "I'm rich. I'm fucking rich."

The trader was about to walk in and get a taste of the gold. Paine put my hand back and prevented the man from going inside. He shook his head at the guy. The trader looked puzzled but listened to him. The man had good instincts.

The gold was clanging loudly as every watched. Martin heard something coming from his left. He looked up and saw a dragon standing before him. The dragon swooped down and bit the man in half. The dragon tossed its body into the air and set it on fire. You could hear Martin screaming as he was being cooked and eaten alive.

Paine closed the portal and said, "I told him that he could take what he could carry. Turns out he couldn't carry much after all."

Paine is a sick person. The gold was covered in blood. The dragon could have been mentioned. I don't even know what else he might have in there. Does he have a hydra? I mean the list is endless.

Darwin looked at Paine with an "Oh shit" look on his face.

The trader said, "Ummm thanks for your business."

Paine replied, "I'm not done yet. I'm here for an army. I plan to get one. Show me your best stock."

The trader was hesitant to help. He just saw a man get eaten by a dragon but realized that not helping would be worse. He took us to the back and walked us to the section that looked like the most dangerous people around. Beings and animals that could slaughter anyone they felt like. Most of them were villains who had to pay their penance for their crimes. They were right up Paine's mindset.

We went by a cage that had a little girl, a black woman, and a Latin man. The trader walked us by them and I noticed he shifted to the left by quite a bit. These two were far more dangerous than the rest. Just like I was drawn to the hyenas for their dangerous nature. Paine was drawn to this group.

Paine said, "I will take both of these individuals."

The trader said, "Are you sure? I have had three returns so far. Two of them last limbs just owning them."

The little girl was taken out of the cage. She had to be eight years old. The little girl was trying to run to the black woman. She seemed to find safety in her. Paine wasn't a man who would harm a child, but he understood that to control them was to control what drove them.

Paine said, "Get these two ready. I want them bathed and ready to go. They look like fun to me."

The black woman looked at him like he was a monster. Darwin was looking closely at what was going on. There was no reason for him to want any of them. The first chance they had, he would be slaughtered. Or so the slaves thought.

Paine walked into the slave auction. There seemed to be only one child and it was the girl in the cage. The slave trader announcer said, "This is Megan. She is eight years old and hasn't had her cherry popped yet."

The crowd laughed a bit. Paine stood there and had a smile on his face. I felt so dirty being here, but Paine was right. My father has more slaves than we can count. I just wish I knew Paine's intentions with them. Was he going to boost their power? Or was he going to use them as a shield against bigger foes?

The bidding started for the little girl. The bid started at one hundred gold. She was a cute little Asian-looking girl. The people were admiring her and plotting to do awful things to her. The amount started at a hundred and fifty gold. The group was fighting each other with their paddles. Paine was evaluating her worth.

Paine yelled out, "One thousand gold."

The crowd looked at Paine like he was crazy. He could have easily paid five hundred gold and beat everyone there, but that wasn't the point. Paine wanted to show that he was in charge and had the gold to back it up.

The announcer verified that he won and grabbed her by the right arm. Paine yelled, "Don't touch her! I don't want a single bruise on her!"

The girl sheepishly walked toward Paine. Loraine knew that Paine was a little rough around the edges and walked to the girl picking her up. She carried her to the front desk area. The other two slaves were let out of their cages and brought to the front.

Michael stayed at the front because he didn't like watching the horrible things happen to people. It was a weird pet peeve of his. Nothing changed with him about that. When he saw a victim, he would want to kill the violators. Michael had a hard time going in to witness.

Michael saw the little girl and wasn't sure why he bought a young girl. His heart sank as he realized that she was a slave and could have been violently used by the men he saw walk back there. His eyes turned purple.

I said, "Put the purple back in the box. There will be no bloodshed today."

The collars were removed by the trader and new ones were put on. Paine put his blood into the new collars and each of them became his. He reached into the Void Storage and pulled out a bunch of gold. The portal was just big enough to fit his arm in.

The trader said, "That will be twelve hundred gold."

I asked, "Why are they so cheap?"

The trader said, "These two keep maiming my guys. I put inhibitors on them, but they still try to kill them. One guy tried to fuck her and his dick went missing. You got your hands full. I hope you know how to deal with slaves."

Paine said, "I know how to deal with them on a personal level."

Well, that sounded ominous. I had no idea what he was thinking, but as soon as he paid the trader. The black woman shot a large piece of ice right through his chest. The ice-covered about ninety percent of his chest and launched him into the air. The ice was so large that it kept him off the ground. Paine's body was stiff and dangling making it look like he was the top part of the letter t. He was breathing still and shoot out breath vapor.

The black woman yelled, "Megan run!"

Megan tried to make her way out the door, but Loraine picked her up and held her closely. The little girl resembled Loraine in looks as if it was her as a little girl. Loraine wouldn't let Megan go and instead held her as close as she could. At that moment, I realized. He didn't buy her for her skills, but because he was trying to give Loraine something. Paine gave Loraine a little girl that the two of them could raise together.

The black woman dropped to her knees. This was the end for them. She tried to kill Paine. The collars would go off and all of them would die. I wasn't sure what her full plan was, but suicide might have been it. Might have been a better choice than being destroyed slowly by a monster.

Michael said, "What did you do that for?"

Paine slowly got up and the icicle in his chest was melting and breaking. The heat and the pressure were showing blood forming into the large icicle. The cracks were slowly breaking until the ice tips broke off. All that was left was the ice inside as his chest closed up.

Paine smiled and said, "That was refreshing. Thanks for that. What's your name?"

The black woman said, "My name is Onyx."

Onyx was in complete fear. Her knew owner just healed right though a death wound as if it was nothing. The shock on her face made her dread anything else in the future. I could see she was trying to figure out in her head whether to kill herself or escape. Either way, death was inevitable in both cases.

Paine replied, "That is a beautiful name. Just like you. I will deal with this indiscretion later. Right now we are leaving this place hopefully in one piece."

The trader said, "Good luck. You're going to need it."

Matilda looked into her eyes and smacked her across the face. She said, "You ungrateful bitch. He paid good money for you and this is the way you treat him."

Paine said, "This is my problem. I'll deal with her in my own way. Don't touch any of my slaves."

Darwin said, "I can't believe you bought a fucking nigger."

Paine just ignored him. That was a really weird thing to say. He was black as well. Why wouldn't he buy more than one? I looked at a mirror on the wall and saw my red hair, freckles, and pointy ears. I was half-Mexican in my past life. God might actually have a sense of humor if I'm right.

The group walked outside and law the sun was going down. The heat was at its peak but was going to cool down from now on. We needed to find an inn that could hold all of us. The day was long. I mean we left the breeding grounds about eighteen hours ago. It was weird that it was still bright outside. I didn't think this place had a nighttime.

The group went to the large building that was an inn. We knew it was an inn because there was a wooden sign on the outside that said inn. It wasn't complicated. The place had four floors worth of rooms.

I walked up to the counter and asked for enough rooms for everyone. The woman said, "You want the top floor. The room has ten beds in it."

I said, "That would be perfect how much."

The woman was looking at me before telling the price. The room was probably fifty silver a night, but since all the other inns were filled up. I knew she was going to overcharge for the room.

The woman said, "One gold a night."

The woman had a smile on her face while saying it. I didn't think it was a scam per se. I was thinking this place looks like it doesn't do enough business to stay afloat. I pulled out ten gold coins. I lay them on the counter spinning the one coin.

I said, "I will take your room for ten nights. I want you to give my friends and me the best experience that you can. If you try to rob us we will kill you all."

Michael said, "I'm sure she can be trusted. Why would someone rob us from this fine establishment."

Michael liked to follow my lead on things. He put on his Hell Armor quickly and looked at the woman. She recognized that he was a demon of some kind. The people showed us to our room. That's right one room filled with beds, but had some extra things that the others didn't like a tub on the end to wash up.

I have never slept in the same room with Michael before. Even though there are so many more people. I was a little nervous. I used X-ray and saw he slept naked a lot. I shouldn't be peaking into what boys do, but he did some strange things and there is a little girl here now.

The group went up to the room and it was huge. The place covered the whole floor. The tub had a cloth around it and was larger than a jacuzzi. I was definitely going to like this. The tub was going to make me feel at home. We each found a bed.

Paine's slaves just stood there waiting to be told if they were getting a bed or not. I don't know how normal slaves worked, but the ones at home were self-sufficient. The cat people licked themselves every day.

The people at the inn brought up hot water in wooden buckets. Loraine saw that Megan was filthy. I took her over to the bath. I took off Megan's clothes and put her in first. She had a look of pain at first but sat in it. The cloth curtain was closed so I stripped down and jumped in with her. Matilda stripped down on the other side of the curtain and walked around. I guess she had the body for it so why not.

Onyx just waited for an invitation. Loraine placed her hand on Onyx's shoulder and said, "They didn't give you a proper cleaning, did they? Come join us. This is a family."

The concept of family seemed to scare her more than a slave. The girl has some psychological damage. I believe she will fit right in.

Chapter 7

O nce the bath was finished I needed some new clothes. These were filthy from being in a dungeon, smelly from my travels, and damaged from being tossed around like a rag doll in a sandstorm.

I called out, "Paine can you please get us some fresh clothes from the storage."

Paine opened up his storage and pulled out an outfit for me, but also pulled out smaller clothes of mine. He was going to have the little girl wear my old outfits. I couldn't pass up her looking very cute in my outfits from when I was nine.

Matilda got two outfits which was really weird. I realized that Onyx was about the same size as Matilda, but a slightly bustier and thicker ass. I would kill for that ass. Mine just feels so flat.

Onyx grabbed one of Matilda's robes. Oh no, Paine set her up for failure. We got dressed and left the tub area. Matilda got out and had a "I'm going to kill that girl" look on her face.

When we got out the guys already had their shirts off. Michael yelled, "We bonded! Guys this is Chavez! He is a high-powered Fire Mage! He was telling us stories about how he lit some of his prior owners on fire! It was hilarious! He did promise not to set Paine on fire for now. Says we seem cool."

Onyx said, "Is that so?"

Onyx scowled at him. I think they had some sort of agreement together to take down anyone that bought them. Onyx was kind of a cold-hearted bitch at times, but she grew on me.

Chavez said, "I just got a feeling. There is something special going on here. Nobody is eyeing you up like a piece of meat. These people are all high-powered heroes which is something we aren't used to. I truly believe they could kill us in a heartbeat, but want us for something."

The guys went into the bath and were splashing the water everywhere. There was enough soap to go around but kept fighting over a small bar. The floor was flooded and I would be surprised if the people down below didn't feel a trickle of water from up above. Men can be such savages at times.

Everyone got dressed from things in the portal and went to bed. I would think that Paine would want to charge his armor for the big day. I wonder why he didn't. The man is wearing the same clothes as Michael all day and night. I just hope he has a plan.

The lights were out the slaves were at the end beds. I was trying to sleep but had a hard time. I was still awake and saw a figure right in front of Paine's bed. I can't believe Loraine is trying to fuck him in a room full of us. Is she crazy?

The figure said, "I will give you my body, just leave the girl alone."

The figure stripped off her clothes. I knew that ass anywhere. Onyx was trying to seduce Paine. She was hard to see in the dark, but I saw her trying to get in bed with a half-awake Paine.

Paine asked, "What the hell are you doing?"

Onyx replied, "I figured if you had me. You would leave Megan alone. That girl is special. Please don't do anything to her."

Loraine woke up and said, "What the fuck is going on?"

The entire room woke up and saw Onyx naked next to Paine in bed. The confusion was that Paine wasn't into sexual stuff. Matilda was looking angry. Onyx was breathing heavily. She wasn't sure what to do. The entire group was seeing her naked in the dark. I think she wanted to cover up, but stood her ground instead.

Michael said, "Looks like you got a little jungle fever. You go boy."

Paine replied to Onyx, "I'm not a pedophile. I'm not into little girls. I love Loraine. She is the closest thing I will ever have to a wife. We grew up together and have an unbreakable bond. I chose you because the men feared the two of you. I chose Megan because she has latent holy energy and will probably be a priestess when she turns nine. Megan also looks like a child Loraine and I could have in this world. I don't wish to bring kids into the world, but having any ally we could raise together is the next best thing. This party is being put together for one purpose. We are going to destroy the Demon Lord."

Onyx asked, "What about the racist shitbag?"

Paine said, "Darwin is a crafter that I plan to use to the fullest. I didn't want a damn Portal Master. I wanted a powerful crafter. He is weak now, but I plan to build him up and show him blueprints of the many things that were drawn up from the last world. If I'm right we will have tanks, nuclear weapons, laser guns, and vehicles that will take us through the desert in air conditioning."

Onyx replied, "You really have blueprints for all that stuff."

Paine said, "I do. Now go to sleep. We have a long day tomorrow."

Onyx threw her robe back on and went to her own bed. The woman was in shock that there were good men. I don't think she ever dealt with a good man in her entire life. I heard her crying in her pillow until she went to sleep.

I went to sleep shortly after she was done making all that racket. I felt like I had five minutes of sleep as the sun came out and blinded me in my eyes. I hated this place. I hate the sun here. The sand is always stuck in my vagina. I'm always thirsty and everyone is in a bad mood trying to smile their agitation away.

I got up and looked like crap. My red hair was everywhere and I didn't have a comb. I hated elven hair. It was so hard to keep under control. The elven girls on television back in the first world always had long flowing hair that made them into beautiful and sought-after women. Why did I get the one mother who had hair in her face every moment of the day?

I looked around and people were already up. The staff in this place brought us some breakfast. Since we were overcharged by a lot. I think they wanted to accommodate us. They did their best to make us feel like royalty. I did wonder since I was actual royalty why we didn't stay in the damn castle. We each could have gotten a servant and had our own room. I was so angry with myself for not bringing it up.

The food was good. A lot better than I anticipated. They gave the boys steak to eat for breakfast. Maybe I was looking at this place all wrong. The reason the room was open was because it was so expensive, but the people here gave five-star service. I shouldn't have judged a book by its cover.

Paine reached into his portal and pulled out a blueprint. Looked like the schematics for a handgun. The pieces and how to make them. Even the bullet type was in the right bottom corner.

Paine said, "Darwin come here. You see this. Are you able to make this?"

Darwin walked over to Paine and looked at the blueprint. I don't think he heard the conversation last night because he was in shock to see a blueprint. Blueprints for things from the other world were very rare. One blueprint could go for ten thousand gold depending on what it was.

Darwin stared at the blueprint. His eye began to turn white. You could literally see in his eyes what he was looking at. Darwin was absorbing all the information. Creationists had to be on a different level of intelligence to make the things they had. One bad piece and sometimes the things would blow up. Being unproperly informed was very dangerous and trying new things without the proper blueprints was a death sentence.

Paine said, "What do you think? Can this be done? I want to see what you are capable of and start small. I want to build you up into a machinist-like class. You could make our lives a whole lot easier if you can."

Darwin pulled off his new shirt and folded it nicely on the table. The tavern owner looked over afraid there might be a brawl about to occur. He closed his eyes and reached into his chest. A small spring came out. Darwin was struggling with each piece. He didn't have mana like the rest of us.

I scanned Darwin closely to see what his level was. He was a level one. The owner made things hard on him by not allowing him to be blessed. The guy is nineteen and hadn't a blessing in ten years.

I said, "Paine he is a level one."

Paine said, "I figured as much. The trick is to get him into a blessing before the fight. I asked around already and tomorrow is the next blessing. I figured we could all do it."

Megan was eating pancakes. She didn't want to hear what everyone was saying. Megan just knew that she was hungry and was a growing girl. Loraine sat with her and had her arm around her. Megan might not have been her biological child, but Loraine loved her as if it was her own.

Matilda said, "If we are attacked today, this guy will have fucking wasted our time."

Loraine called Matilda out, "There is a little girl here! Watch what you say!"

Matilda's nose flared out and exclaimed, "FUCK FUCK FUCK FUCK YOU!"

Michael said, "That's enough Matilda she is right. Not around the little girl. At least until she gets her blessing."

Matilda really had a problem with being a team player and doing the right thing. She had a weird thing about control. I wouldn't be surprised if she was plotting our father's death as we speak so she can claim the crown.

Chavez raised his hand into the air. He acted like we were in grade school. I pointed at him to speak. Chavez had a smirk on his face. I wasn't sure if he was going to have a wise-ass comment.

Chavez asked, "What are we to do? You bought the four of us and we are lost on your plan for us."

Paine said, "Megan is too young to fight, but I don't want her in the city when the riots occur. The seven of you will be on the tower walls by the gate. Your goal is to prevent them from getting into the city as a backup in case my plan fails. Loraine and Megan's protection is the utmost priority. Matilda and Isabella, you would just get in their way. Michael and I will be in the front of the gate. We will raise some hell."

Onyx said, "You do realize that they will surround the castle and try to break in. I can't see them sending eighteen million troops to one location."

Paine replied, "I am depending on that."

The group was silent and just ate their food. The slaves didn't want to argue with him because he was their master. I believe most of the time when the slaves attacked their masters. They had a justified reason.

Darwin finished making his gun but was really winded. His head was on the table and looked like he was about to fall asleep. The gun was finished, but that was just the start in Paine's eyes. He was going to see what Darwin was capable of.

Paine handed me the gun and said, "Hold this we are about to test him out."

Paine picked up Darwin and carried him out of the tavern dropping some coin for the meal. The look on the owner's face was stunned as he left way too much money again. I don't think he even asks how much his meal is.

The group went up to the farms and went to the wall. There was space for people to drive through if they needed to. Paine dropped his body in the dirt. The group wasn't sure what we were doing here. Darwin woke up and I handed him the gun. There were no rounds in the gun at all.

Paine said, "Guess what Darwin. You get to shoot me."

Darwin responded, "What are you talking about? There are no bullets in this gun."

Paine said, "That is not a gun. It is a weapon. The same as a spear or sword. You know how to make the rounds for it, The rounds were in the corner of the blueprint. Don't worry I put the blueprint away. I didn't want you drooling all over it."

Darwin asked, "Okay, and made a bullet that came out of his chest."

Paine said, "What the fuck are you doing?"

Loraine replied, "Watch your language. Little girl sitting right here!"

Paine apologized immediately. He was still getting used to the fact that he had a kid now. Paine closed his eyes and tried to think of how to explain things. He was going to try making the comparison to his own powers.

Paine said, "You know the material comes out of your chest. There is a fixed location in which you gain the stuff. I can form a Void Sphere in my hand. That is the easiest way to make a sphere, but I can also make one at a distance."

Paine raised his right arm and formed a Void Sphere twenty feet away. He closed it immediately after to show that distance wasn't a factor, but didn't want to accidentally kill someone that was driving through. Poor horses wouldn't stand a chance.

Paine said, "You get what I'm saying. Form the bullets into the gun and just fire until you run out of mana. Loraine is right here ready to form a mana well if you need."

Darwin was shaking. I could not see this going well. He needed to put the ammo in the right way and fire off a round. This was quite a dangerous endeavor because if he made a round wrong. It could blow off his hand or backfire and shoot him in the face.

Darwin closed his eyes and pulled the trigger. A round came out and hit the wall. Paine was pleased and walked over to the wall. He wanted to get hit by the rounds. Paine made the shoot-me gesture. Darwin was hesitant but saw Paine take a giant icicle through the chest. Darwin pulled the trigger and shot him in the chest.

Paine reacted and yelled, "You shot me. I can't believe you actually shot me."

Paine fell to the ground and played dead. He was messing with Darwin. Darwin looked at his gun and had that look of what did I just do. He told me to do it. Darwin was trying to explain away everything that just happened and threw the gun on the ground. His hands were shaking worse than a man with Parkinson.

Paine lifted his head and said, "Would it have been easier if I was a nigger? Eventually, I will get rid of that worthless mindset."

Paine got off the ground and dusted himself off. Darwin stayed silent. He looked at the ground. He realized he was a black man who hated his own kind. Nobody actually knew what caused him to be this way. I thought a KKK member, but he completely denied it. The man seemed more confused than anything.

Darwin picked up the gun and was enraged. He shot round after round. There was no stopping him. Each bullet hit Paine. There was blood running down his chest and two in the head. Paine was embracing each blow as if it was nothing. This went on for five minutes until the fatigue set in and he put a round in the chamber backwards. The round shot out the back of the gun and missed his face by a cunt hair.

All we heard was a man crying out behind us. "What just happened?! My ass, my ass! Someone just stabbed me in the ass!"

Paine looked around. The bullets were falling out of his chest. He walked down the road and waved his arm for us to come with him. Paine was whistling as if that didn't draw attention toward us.

The group was really becoming unison as Paine was really becoming the leader of the group. It took me a while, but he was always leading the charge. Picking out locations. Coming up with plans. Buying slaves and I was following him every step of the way. I'm ashamed to admit it, but he was good at it too.

Paine grabbed Darwin by the shoulder. He said, "This next part is probably going to be one the hardest things you will ever do. I have a portal that will lead you to every blueprint that I have ever collected. Your job from now on is to study every one of them and see what you can build before the Blessing occurs."

Darwin agreed because he had no choice. Paine opened his portal and Darwin walked in all alone. It looked like there was a fireplace with a bed and drawers that seemed to carry hard papers inside. I really did feel bad for the guy. Even though he was a racist piece of shit.

We walked back to the room to lay down. Paine took Onyx and Chavez up to the wall to test their powers on the outside. I didn't go since I was tired of being dragged around like a purse. They were out there for an hour before coming back.

I was trying to get some shut-eye. My eyes closed and threw the blankets overtop of me. I enjoyed the sweet quiet as Loraine and Megan were both sleeping as well. The sun was out most of the time. I was getting used to it and drifted off into a slumber.

Paine came in and stomped his feet. I was getting a little pissed off and was about to go over and slap him. He opened his portal and out came Darwin. The poor guy was in there for over an hour. That is sixty years of personal training the guy did. I really hope it was worth it.

Darwin came out screaming. He was used to silence for so long. The noise was like a deaf can hearing for the first time in the middle of Times Square. The city was loud most of the time. His eyes looked like they were about to pop out of his head. Darwin was shrieking as everyone. Paine tried to calm him down. His skin was pale and was having a hard time adapting to his surroundings.

Paine said, "Calm down. Did you memorize all of it?"

Darwin was in shock and said, "I did that twenty years ago. HAHAHAHAHAHAHHA!"

Paine said, "Good, now show me what you built."

Chapter 8

The light was bright, but Darwin knew that he had to do something. He opened his own portal. The inside was pure white and bright. It looked like he made his own portal to store all his gadgets in. Everything was built and stored in this area. The portal wasn't something normally done for Craft Masters, but the garage blueprint helped him accomplish this goal.

I turned over and put the pillow over my face yelling, "People are trying to sleep. Could you shut him up?"

Paine said, "I'm heading to the church tonight you want to come."

I said, "It's not the night to do it yet. That is tomorrow. You want to piss these priests off too."

Paine said, "If we want our weapons to work, we need to maintain them. I have a feeling the goblins will be here tomorrow sometime. They know our rituals and schedules. Let's break the system."

I said, "Fine, Michael you coming."

Michael just sat there daydreaming. I had no idea what he was thinking about, but it seemed strange that he was thinking at all. Michael was always an act first and dealt with the consequence later kind of guy. He even began following Paine around like a lost puppy. It was as if killing the king and Gandriel did something to him.

I walked over to Michael and sat with him. My fingers snapped in front of his face. Michael did not budge an inch. This was rather strange. His eyes were going in and out from turning purple. Something broke his spirit.

I said, "You okay."

Michael replied, "Yeah, I'm just thinking of asking Matilda if she wants to marry me. It's a long shot, but you always lose the chances you don't take right."

I was angry. Why does she get to have Michael? This seemed unfair. I fought for him for so long that I just got friend-zoned. I guess it was never meant to be. I was really sad about it, but Matilda finally won. I hated that she always won.

I said, "Go for it. Not like anyone else would want you."

I walked out the door with Paine and the rest of the group. Michael was left in the room all alone. I think he was seriously depressed as well. I shouldn't have said that to him, but I was mad. He eventually got to the church with us.

Matilda said, "These shitbags better let us in or I will burn this bitch down."

Matilda was becoming problematic. She was trying to gain control of the group, but couldn't outshine Paine. That made Paine a prime target and she did her best to seduce him. It wasn't working though as Paine saw through her and loved Loraine.

Darwin managed to calm down after a while. His eyes kept shifting back and forth for a while. He sat down in the pew. I sat next to him and Onyx was on the other side. Darwin tried to seem crazy for a while. I noticed though that he kept looking over at Onyx. Something happened in the Void Storage. He kept looking at the back of his hand and staring at her.

I realized something was off. Darwin didn't seem to look at her in a hateful way anymore. I believe that he was looking in the mirror every day that Paine placed specifically in the room. The mirror was weird as I smashed it a few times, but came right back together.

Paine made him look at his reflection to see what kind of man he truly was and began to hate himself. It took sixty years for that hate to be set aside and accept who he was.

Darwin was a very complicated man, but never scorned Onyx for being black ever again. In fact, this was the moment that he admired her from afar. He gained interest in her as she had skin smoother and darker than anyone he ever met. His hatred drew to fascination. That curiosity led him to fall in love with her. To him it was sixty years. To her, it was hours ago. She still remembers him as the man he used to be. This was going to be a long journey for him to gain her affections.

One of the priests came out to greet us. His ropes were white and gold with a black trim around the neck. The robes weren't very clean and didn't look like he had washed them in several days. This was very different from the priests in Tryanon as they bought a new robe every week.

He asked, "How can I help you?"

Paine came forward and said, "I am a paladin from the church in Tryanon. You can say I was a lucky person as one of the survivors of the massacre. I came to help you with these comrades to fight against the goblin horde coming this way."

The priest said, "So the rumors are true. They are coming. Have you come to pray?"

Paine said, "Yes we all have in your courtyard where we believe God will hear us the loudest."

The priest replied, "You can, but the new moon isn't until tomorrow. I'm afraid it will just end up being prayers tonight."

Paine responded with, "I know this, but we have come to ask God to hear our pleas for help. We need the strength to get through this battle and know that we can't do it alone."

The priest nodded his head. These priests are oblivious to what is going on. I truly believe they didn't realize that you can be blessed every night. If this was the case, why wouldn't it work during the day? I know what you're thinking plot twist they will do it during the day because of what Isabella said. It never happens during the day. It was just a legitimate question.

The group waited in the pew until it got dark. Michael walked in to join us. The church filled up as many people heard the rumors and came to pray. When tragedy is about to strike. The fearful come out and look to a higher power to save them, always.

The group went into the back of the church. The courtyard had sand throughout it. Since the children weren't demanded to clean it every day. The church didn't look as nice. There is always a small cost for kindness.

Darwin was the first to go up for a prayer. We all agreed he needed it the most. Poor guy wasn't blessed in ten years. His heart was ready for a change. With everything that was thrown at him, life is always harder without a good Blessing.

Light shined down from the sky on Darwin. Darwin rose into the air. Holy energy was spreading him out as he floated on his back. Lightning struck down on him. His energy was flowing and surrounding his body. Sparks were flying everywhere like when Michael first got his. He was crying out in pain as each bolt pierced his body and soul.

Darwin fell slowly to the ground. The first person that came to his aid was Onyx. She seemed truly worried about him. That was a shock to the rest of us. His shirt was torn to shreds and the pink scars on his back were showing for all to see. Her hatred simmered down as she watched him suffer again. The ice queen once again showed she had a heart after all.

The rest of the group went to aid Darwin. I used this time to enter the circle. I needed to grow as a person. I needed God's strength for the incoming battle. This was my last shot. I didn't skip or dance. This was a moment that made me grow as a person.

I looked up and a bright light shined on me. The Void was around me. I saw no forest. Sylvia and Diego were right next to me. In the distance, was a flashing bright light. We followed the light to its source. I wasn't sure what to expect. Usually, there was a forest that I would use the stars to navigate.

Angela came down and lit up the land. I was in my childhood home with my mother. She was crying her eyes out. The dishes were being washed, but my mother never did the dishes. This had to be an illusion.

I asked, "What is this supposed to be? What am I seeing?"

Angela said, "This was the moment that your mother let herself feel emotion again. Your father died that morning. Believe it or not, your father was one of two men that she loved with all her heart. Both men died tragically because of her. At least, that's the way she saw it. Look the key is in the door to prove it."

I walked over to my room and indeed the key was there. The paint on the door was close to the same as I remembered. I walked through the door and saw myself lying there in bed trying to sleep. I had tears running down my face. I was so cute back then. I was tanner than I remembered. My face did resemble my mother's by quite a bit. I think she hated me because she hated herself. My eyes were like my father's.

I felt pain in my chest. This was the Void. I was next to Angela. Why was I feeling pain? These things were old news. I walked to the window and noticed a masked figure climb the fire escape. When things were slowed down, I could properly see. I got right in the masked figure's face. Holy shit, it was the case worker Jamie.

I said, "This can't be real. Is this what really happened for is this what my mind perceives happened."

Angela responded, "This is what really happened. You have stunted your growth. Your focus seemed to be on how to get what you want. You are being blessed by quite a bit. God chose to give you a rare ability that very few have seen. Your mother from Kepogle is a shining star in an endless wilderness. Her bloodline has blessed you well."

I asked, "Is that the place in Mexico she was from?"

Angela said, "No, Kepogle is the planet you are currently on."

Wow, I just learned something. People kept calling it the second world. Who knew that it had an actual name. The room began to change. I was outside the Peterson's home. The tree was still looking good. I crawled up into it one last time and watched the sun start to set.

Angela walked over to me and watched it with me. She, too, marveled at the things God created. The way the light hit the ground made me feel something inside. I looked over and saw a car drive up.

I wished I never met him. Levi changed my life forever. He had that look to him that reminded me of the man I truly loved. The man who seems to prefer my sister over me. Why was my life always feeling like a constant amount of regret?

I wanted to cry but had no tears to give. That boy was my first kill. I have to wonder now. If I hadn't met him, would I be in heaven right now? Am I hear because my heart was dedicated to killing people and not towards God.

Angela and I watched as Levi brought me back after that horrible night. Diego and Sylvia were watching and feeling my personal pain. I wasn't sure why I was seeing these images again. Why was this so important?

I asked, "What is the purpose of this?"

Angela answered, "Because sometimes we need to look back and see how we have grown. It doesn't happen overnight. You have become a remarkable young woman. In time, you will see that Michael sees that in you too."

The room changed again. This time I was with my mother. I had to be eight months old. My father was standing there with me in his arms. He looked so happy. My mother was in a wooden rocking chair. They had another baby that looked just like me. I was a twin. How did I not know this? There is another sister of mine out there. A pure-blood elf looked at my mother. He told her she had to go.

My mother was told to leave by the elves. One child was brought with her to the elven village and the other stayed with my father. I stayed with my father to be raised as royalty. I wondered what kind of life my sister led. Is she stronger or weaker than me? I had a hard time containing my joy.

Angela said, "There is so much more, but we can go through that at a later date."

I asked, "What if there isn't a later date?"

Angels replied, "Even in death, there is always a later date. With the gift of the Kaiju, I don't see you dying this coming day. Help the new recruits to grow and fight together. You just might need them to survive."

I said, "What is that supposed to mean?"

Angela started to float away. Her feathers were falling from the sky blinding me. I could no long see her. This was crap. I needed to ask her what I would need these people for. What does she know? Am I even part of the end of the story?

I cried out, "Get back here and answer me! This is my time!"

Diego smiled at me and got in my face. He said, "Your time is up. Now it's our turn to guide you once again. Bond us. We are ready. We are one with the hyenas. This is the point where we no longer need to guide you but form a pact with you."

I asked, "What do you mean pact with me?"

Diego was on my left and Sylvia was on my right. They held me in the air. I was floating in the air far beyond anything I thought possible. My chest felt like it was caving in. I could feel something I didn't think would happen. I felt FEAR of the fairies. I was risen into the air as they looked into my eyes. Their force. Their very being was being sucked into my hands and becoming part of me. My hyenas appeared before me. I could see them in my shirt pocket small as can be.

I felt a power unlike I have ever before. The hyenas were my family, my pack, and I was their alpha. My eyes glowed red and my red hair grew high spreading throughout the air. My hair was like a maze of guidance that allowed me to transcend normal thought and reality. My Passive Scan activated as I collapsed to the ground. This was not normal. I dropped down and landed on my feet barely feeling the impact. My eyes created red lightning around them.

I felt alive. As I walked forward my hair was so long that it dragged on the ground like a wedding dress train. I saw the forest once again, but this time nothing felt like it was in my way. I walked forward and walked on the very air that I believed to be breathing. Each step brought me closer to the top of the waterfall.

I stood before the door, but it refused to open. I knocked on the door. The door would not budge. My nose flared up and my ears got bigger and sharper. I gained my fangs. My hair was flowing through the wind and I was ready to return. What was I forgetting? What was I missing?

Down below at the bottom of the waterfall was my hyenas. My guardians and best friends in this world. The beings that would never hurt me but are bonded to me spiritually for the rest of my life. I jumped off the waterfall onto the ground to retrieve them. My red curly hair worked its way around their large bodies forming a bond.

I knelt down and patted them on the head. Both hyenas lay down and whimpered as they felt the comfort of my warm embrace. My hands held still as my blood transferred through my hair. They could feel my sadness and pain. Their bond with me is permanent. My hair shortened to its normal length and my fangs were gone. The red lightning dissipated and I was ready to leave now.

I turned around and held both of them in my arms. The hyenas nuzzled up to me. Diego through his mouth said, "Let's go. They are waiting on us."

I used my teleportation up to the ledge with them in my arms and the doors opened. We needed to bond in this world before we returned. I don't know what happened, but I felt bigger than ever. My strength was twice what I felt before. It was truly time to leave. The hyenas ran into the portal first ready to guide me and lead the charge. I was no longer going to be prey. I was going to be a permanent predator.

I walked through the door and dropped fast. The world was turning upside down and the stars were by my side twinkling as I fell. The flickering was blinding, but I felt secure like they wouldn't let me get hurt. My body was right there. I flew straight into my second world body. I dropped to the ground hard, leaving a body print on the ground.

I felt my body collapsing under the strenuous amount of weight. The stones below me were crushed and debris flew throughout the courtyard. The dust was settling and people around me stared in shock. Eventually, the dust settled and I felt alone.

I don't know why I felt alone for that moment. Paine was standing right there. Everyone in my group looked like they were getting ready to cheer me on.

Diego came out of my pocket and licked my face. I was having a hard time moving but sat up anyway. I looked back and there was a line. Not just a little line, but every hero in the city waiting to take a turn.

David was standing there pointing and said, "Forget stupid politics, I was never good at it anyway. Your group started this now the city is prepared to be strong. This is going to be the fight of our lives. I hope you guys are ready."

I said, "I was born ready."

Chapter 9

The city banded together and took their turns after us. We traveled to our room and laid down for the evening. David walked us to our room. I wasn't sure why, but I think he wanted to let us know what we were up against.

I just wanted to get some shut-eye. David came in and said to the group, "Do you know what a goblin is? I want to make sure you know what we are up against. Word has it that the goblin forces are gathering and should be in here in ten our. I fought with my brother on how to resolve this and his stupid answer seems to be to keep the treaty somehow and ask what they want. I started this war, and I plan to destroy them before they get to big and destroy us anyway. When our ancestors made the treaty, it was suppose to just protect the people. They needed a way to survive and now they wiped their ass with the treaty and the numbers have blown up to far."

Michael sat up out of his bed and replied, "Enlighten us, David. It may save our lives."

David began the story of how it was believed the goblins came to be. "A beautiful elven woman was down by the river. Her hair glistened in the sun. The warrior spirits before her graced her presence with hair the color of blood.

The elven woman was carrying water to her village. The river was the clearest water in the land. Everyday she would do her chores and bring the water with her. The elven woman was considered wise and beautiful at such a young age. Everyone admired her.

One day a man came to the river to retrieve water himself. He traveled the banks of the river looking for food and water to quench his thirst. The river had the purest water in the land. He could not resist, but to travel and find out for himself why the water was so pure.

The river and everything around it belonged to the elves. The eleven people were suspicious of anyone in the area and would often kill. There was a reason for this as men were killing elves for many generations. Man could not be trusted.

The man was as stranger to the elven people. The elves were ready to battle any man that came across their village. The humans were easily swayed by the devil and the elves did want their perversions in their town.

The elven woman was intrigued because she never met such an interesting-looking man. His ears were sharp and his skin was softer than the finest silk. His teeth acted like fangs but were very kind and sweet. His skin was purple which at the time nobody realized was the mark of a demon. He had a black cloak on that swayed into the wind and created a mysticism about himself.

The elven woman was enticed by the man so she brought him back to the village for the council to learn about him. The council scolded her for a bring back and outsider. They thought bringing a man back to the village would only bring death and remorse. His ways might change the very thoughts that brough them piece and prosperity for many generations.

The demon had a silver tongue and spoke to the elves with poise and grace. He persuaded them to let himself be accepted by them. His evil nature was hidden by the people of the village for quite a few years.

His name was Beelzebub. Beelzebub had aww inspiring wit that charmed the women of the village. Most of the women wanted to be with him. That wasn't good enough for him.

Beelzebub had his eyes set on the only woman that denied him. The woman he met by the water. He grace and beauty emanated. Her hair was like blood which drove him crazy. Her spirit was that of a warrior. The demon was able to recognize real strength.

The elven woman played coy for a long time. She had no interest in the demon. In fact, somethin felt really off, she was repulsed by him. Being the up and coming leader of the elves. The elven woman pushed away his advances.

Beelzebub made his intentions known. He wanted to mate with her. The elven woman could see there was no love coming from him. All he cared about was power and lust. Just like the humans.

Beelzebub made his advances at the elven woman. She denied him three times, but the demon wouldn't take no for an answer. Upon the third rejection, Beelzebub grabbed the elven woman and took her to the Forest of the Mist.

The Forest of the Mist was a location that nobody could see through. The only true inhabitants were the Ents. The Ents were a tribe of living tree beings. Their bark was harder than rocks and spoke slowly. The limbs were able to grow fast and hold anything they wanted into place.

People believe that the Forest of the Mist is Beelzebub's true home. A place where he commands the trees and kills anyone who enters. His speed can't be outmatched.

All species stay clear of the Forest in the Mist because of the great dangers. The Ents that live there have been known to rip a person apart limb by limb. People in the past have been lured into the forest and never to be seen again.

Beelzebub took the elven woman to this exact location. She had fear in her eyes knowing that the stories were of people never leaving this place. He picked her up and threw her over his shoulder like a Barbarian. Beelzebub flew with her to the location of choice.

The elven woman was set down in the forest. Beelzebub asked her to be his mistress. He begged and pleaded for her affections. He wanted to form a family that would bring his own personal version of peace to the word.

The elven woman kept refusing him because she would never mate with a man without marriage. Demons never got married since it was a holy union in front of God. They dismissed everything to do with God.

The elven woman denied his advances. Beelzebub was angry that she wouldn't accept his advances. He couldn't stand it anymore. Beelzebub was a general in the devil's army and nobody was to tell him no.

Beelzebub had the Ents hold her in place. He wanted to see face as he was about to torture her in the worst ways a elf can experience. Beelzebub plan was to break her spirit, but she was strong.

The elven woman's clothes were ripped from her body. She denied Beelzebub many more times. He would lick her, kiss her, and grope her, but nothing was working. Beelzebub after six long days said to her, "You aren't making this easy. I like that but in the end. I am a demon. I don't need your permission."

Beelzebub had the Ents lower her onto the ground. He removed his clothes and raped her mercilessly. He slapped her and beat her. Every inch of him was inside her as he ruthlessly fucked her. An evil deed created an evil seed.

The elven woman had eight children shortly after. Each of the children roamed off to different parts of the world and began a life anew. They found themselves hosts of human women and would break them down for procreation reasons. Each child was a race that we deal with today. Goblins were the runt of the group. Medusai, trolls, minotaur, kobold, Dameoni, Bug bear, and vampires. Other generals formed other children, but Beelzebub made children that spread across the world and became easily one of the great generals."

Michael asked, "What are Dameoni?"

David responded, "Dameoni are a weird hybrid race. They appear as humans but change into dark creatures. Only God can unleash them, but it is found in their blood. A few names have been given to them to seem more normal. Death Knights, Demon Slayers, Blood Mages, et cetera.

These classes are rare beasts. They seem to exhibit human characteristics. I have never met one before so there is no need to be alarmed. I have to admit you fooled me into thinking I met one. Michael, you had me scared for a moment. I truly believed you were one, but your personality isn't the same as a Dameoni. Also, they grow horns, scales, and have wings when they are Demon Slayers. You don't have a single scale on you."

Michael asked, "Are they the strongest race?"

David said, "I think so, which is why they are rare. When one shows up, he will be able to match a true demon and is ten times faster than a Fury Warrior. The fastest class in the world."

Michael had a smirk on his face. He was slowly trying to find out who he was. His ancestors were born from Beelzebub. That would also make him part elf like I am. For the longest time, we kept what he was from him. I think by letting David speak. I fucked that up.

David said, "Want to know more. I have heard all these stories a million times."

Paine knew he was speaking too much, but let him anyway. Paine was an experienced strategist. I think he let him speak to much to further his own agenda. His strategies weren't as good as my father's. I could see quite a few mistakes. Over time, I believe he will surpass my father and be a true diplomat.

Michael realized that everything David said was stuff he was. The horns, scales, and wings are all things he had at one point when he lost control. The realization that you're an ancestor of the devil himself took a toll on him. I didn't pity him in the least.

This does explain why people hated the elven race. If one elf was responsible for the worst races in the world, I would probably hate them too. I couldn't help, but feel my ears. They were really the only true link to my elven ancestors. I let my hair down so people wouldn't notice.

Paine and Loraine seem to know know about my ancestors. Paine was very observant and would watch me play with my ears often. The points on my ears were protruding longer as I got older. I have to wonder if my aging will be human or elven.

Elves live very long lives. My mother could look young and be four hundred years old. The races seems to outlive every human they ever meet. It makes me worry that I might outlive Michael by a lot.

Matilda knows I'm an elf because she met my mother at my birthday. The way she treats me always made we wonder if she knew my mother before my ninth birthday. She was only two at the time, but didn't seem very surprised to see her at my birthday party.

I don't know if Michael doesn't know. He is wierd about things and would probably say something stupid. Michael has his moments when he sees everything around him to the greatest of details. The next he doesn't realize I'm not wearing shoes.

All I can say about our relationship is that I don't want Michael to know that I'm an elf. I'm afraid he may hate me. Even though his ancestors were elves. The devil side my hate elves. I don't want his devil side to come out and hurt me when he realizes what I am.

There were always secrets in this group. Paine doesn't talk about his past. I'm an elf. Michael wasn't supposed to know he was a demon. Matilda well, I always feel like there is a dark secret with her.

I never asked Matilda because she might actually tell me. There is a darkness lurking inside her that would make the demons blush. I can sense it but don't bring it up because I would just look jealous since she is Michael's favorite.

I went to bed and fell asleep. Soon enough there is going to be war. I am not looking forward to this. Hopefully, by the time we are done. The whole species will be annihilated. I was tossing and turning in my sleep. The nightmares usually don't get to me anymore, but my eyes didn't want to sleep. I was fearing that I was getting insomnia from the light all the damn time.

Before I knew it, it was daytime. The group was getting around. Paine came over to me and said, "Here is a new bow and knives for you. I sense they will do you better than your current weapons. These are designed to match your spirit aura. A gift Darwin has now."

I grabbed the weapons. The bow felt lighter than a feather. The knives had no weight to them at all. The bow was set next to my bed. I had to see if the knives were sharp.

My left pointer finger was getting close to the blade when it cut my finger. I hadn't even touched the tip yet. There seemed to be an aura around the blade that reminded me of the Star Sparks on the arrows when I shoot them. It might have been the weapons or it might have been me leveling up. Either way. This was hardcore.

I put my straps on my wrists and hands. It always helped me grip the bow and prevent backlash damage. Michael walked over to me and looked into my eyes. I was thinking he was going to say something stupid like he always does.

Michael said, "You should let your ears be shown. I think they are kind of cute. Kind of."

Michael walked away acting like he was cool. My hair would get in the way while I was firing the bow. I don't know why this is such a hard decision to make. Hair up or hair down. Why am I caring what people think anyway? Being a girl sucks sometimes.

I made a battle decision. My hair went up into a ponytail. It looked awful since my hair was so curly, but I didn't care. At least not at this very moment. I put the bow over my right shoulder and picked up my quiver. It was time for war.

Paine said, "Since it looks like we are ready. I want to take a moment to see if I can motivate you. This battle will suck. I mean really suck. People will lose their lives. That is the nature of a war. I don't see myself dying today. I know this because I haven't figured out how after my many attempts to kill myself. The rest of you will have to watch each other's backs.

The group is going to welcome our new recruits. They aren't just my slaves, but my family. You will treat them with dignity and not get them killed. They were expensive."

Michael laughed and said, "They cost less than your wardrobe for the month."

Paine said, "Not now you pompous ass. I'm on a roll. I am here to tell you that these people depend on us. In the first ten minutes of the battle. Michael and I will probably die or be immobilized. I'm hoping it's immobilized. Your job is going to be to kill whatever is left.

I can see an army of trolls coming to their aid. We have all experienced trolls I'm sure. They are nothing to fuck with. If by some miracle we all survive at the end of the day. I will do the unthinkable."

Michael responded, "Nobody wants to see your tiny dick."

Paine shook his head and said, "I was going to give each of you a hug."

Michael smiled and said, "Sorry bud, I don't want your erection hugs. I know it will be the highlight of the evening for you, but not my thing."

Paine replied, "I'm not gay! Whatever! You get nothing then! I might just fart on your pillow and give you pink eye, Michael!"

Michael laughed. He realized that the speech was a downer and Paine wasn't good at making people laugh. Everyone has their gifts. Michael had a gift for building morale through humor. I actually think Paine liked it. He once mentioned a guy like him in his prior life.

Paine said, "I lost my train of thought. Ummm you know what fuck it. Just get on the wall. We are going to go to Pound Town and kill these guys."

Michael yelled, "Giggity!"

The room laughed. Paine looked lost. He thought the phrase meant to beat a guy up. The actual meaning is well... If you didn't understand the meaning then you are probably too young to read this book.

The group walked out of the inn. Paine was leading the way. The streets were filled with people. There was no applauding. The people just stared at us like we were crazy for taking on that many goblins. I saw fear in their eyes.

Michael thought the people were showing support and waved at them. He had a smile on his face and his hand was going back and forth weirdly. He was breathing heavily. I think his goal was to show the people no fear.

Michael said, "Wave to the people."

I said, "You look ridiculous. What kind of a wave is that anyway?"

Michael replied, "It was the pageantry wave. I remember watching the pageants on television because of my one foster mother. The girls waved like this."

I recognized it now. His wave was stiffer than the girls on the television. He looked more like an alien or a robot. When he smiled I don't think he realized this. His fangs were showing. That would scare people off even worse.

Matilda looked at him and said, "Knock that shit off. People need to see us as strong right now. They are scared and you look like a moron."

Michael put his hand down. His eyes turned purple and lightning was coming off of him a little bit. He was trying to hide his powers. He turned them off immediately and looked around. I didn't notice what he did right away. Maybe he had control and thought something through. Michael has been doing better at this lately.

Nope, I spotted it. Michael took Matilda's robe and turned it inside out and backward. He changed it so that everyone could see her ass through the center of the robe. It was definitely funny, but very very juvenile. I was holding back my laughter.

Matilda was pissed. She said, "Michael put it back this moment."

Michael responded, "Whatever do you mean? I'm just back here with Isabella. Isabella, did you see me move at all?"

Matilda had her hands behind her trying to cover her ass. I nodded no since I actually didn't see him move a muscle toward her. I hope she doesn't kill one of us during the battle. The look in her eyes was that of the devil himself.

We finally made it to the castle gates. There was a stairway on both sides of the gate. The wall was over a thousand feet tall so there were only two ways to get in. Through the wall, which was constantly being repaired by Nature Mages. Sometimes the heroes would call them Earth Mages since it was a call back to the first world.

The only real way to get into the down was to go over the wall or through the gate. To go over the wall, you would need towers or thousand foot ladders We would destroy them before they even showed up.

The soldiers and I were going up the stairwell. The walk was long. I wasn't feel the length like I usually do. Once at the top, I took Diego and Sylvia out of my pocket. They were glowing and looked like they were trying to fuse with my body.

The hyenas turned into their normal forms scarring the shit out of the archers. They were about fifteen feet at the time. Their size took of over half the area we were standing at the wall.

The soldiers were afraid of my babies. Hyenas were some of the most untamable aggressive animals in the kingdoms. I had two. I think quite a few of the soldiers ended up pissing their pants.

Diego and Sylvia peeked over the wall. The drop was long and the soldiers were afraid to get too close to the edge.

The wind was picking up so it was hard to see what was in the distance. I didn't see a single goblin. I wondered if they were even coming today. Maybe they weren't going to come at all.

I sat down as Matilda was chanting. She had lightning around her eyes. The sky was turning black and darkness covered the land. Her version of prep time was laying down a storm upon the battlefield.

Last time there was a mission like this for Matilda. She dropped a meteor killing thousands of these guys to save a small village. This would be thousands of times more than last time. She wanted her sweet kills.

The sand storms were getting worse or so it seemed. I scanned the distance and behold. It wasn't the weather this time. The marching of the goblins was covering the desert and shaking it up. Most people couldn't see what was going on.

Paine jumped off the side of the wall with no armor on. Michael and him both were just wearing those black clothes that Wong kept making them.

Michael looked at me. I could see something was bothering him as he looked at me. I knew something needed to be said. Michael looked like he wanted to say something, but chose not to.

I walked over to him before he jumped off and yelled, "Michael! I love you!"

Michael said, "I know."

Michael did a swan dive off the wall disappearing into the sands. It was so hard to see with all the winds my sister was stirring up. I hated him for that, but before we might die I said my peace.

Chapter 10

Lightning was collecting through the sky. The city had never seen darkness that thick before. Even during the harshest of sand storms, the land never got this dark. I was having a hard time breathing. This was by far the most dangerous thing we had ever done. It wasn't even for my own kingdom.

David and Augustus came to the wall. They brought with them a third. The man had a twirled mustache with black hair. His robes were black with gold stars throughout the designs. He had on shoes that were black and curved upward at the toe. His height was close to mine and looked to be in his early twenties.

Augustus said, "With all the king's horses and all the king's men. We will never let this wall fall again."

David said, "Solomon don't go nuts and say stupid shit like him."

The man in the black clothes was the third brother Solomon. Solomon said, "Looks like I have another brother here. I wonder how advanced he is."

I have no idea what he was talking about. I was listening to Paine. He told Michael to dig a two-foot trench around the city. Michael went into his speed form and went to work. What the hell was he planning? It was like he was plowing a field around the the city wall.

Megan looked over the wall and she was amazed at the sight. She had never seen anything like this before in her life. We had to bring her with us since the town may riot in fear. I expected there to be quite a bit of looting while the guards are occupied.

Chavez was hugging Onyx and said, "We will get through this. This is the first time in our lives that we will get to fight for a good cause. These people are different. They feed us well and have tried to help us grow. We have to fight this fight. If anything, for Megan's sake."

Onyx looked like she was going to cry. Most of the time she puts on a tough girl routine, but I think she is soft deep down in her own way. Onyx was given the name Ice Queen by the people in the slave trade. I think they just pushed her over the edge.

Michael took his swords and created a large dug-out track around the city. Michael said, "Now what are we going to do."

Paine said, "Now you need to defend me. What I am about to do is going to take a lot out of me. I need total focus or we will both die."

Paine pulled his armor from the Void Storage and placed it next to him. He also grabbed a large dagger from the storage and had it placed firmly in his right hand. Paine used his left hand and put his shirt in the storage.

Paine closed his eyes and exclaimed, "Blood Ritual!"

Paine took the knife and stabbed himself in the stomach. The blood was pouring out of him and traveling along the ditch that Michael had just made. He just kept stabbing himself over and over again trying to get as much blood out of him as possible.

Michael asked, "Are you going to do what I think you are? The city is too big. You're going to kill yourself."

Paine laughed and replied, "Then so beat it. My life wasn't worth much to begin with. If I'm going to die. I want it to mean something."

Paine kept stabbing himself spitting up blood and working its way around the city. The goblins got close enough for us to see. They just stood there waiting for the signal. The goblins were in such unison that their left feet dropped at the exact same time. It was terrifying to see them as a hive mind.

Paine wasn't deterred at all. He kept spilling blood trying to cover the whole outside. The goblins brought wyvern to the battle. There had to be thousands of them flying in the air with a goblins riding them.

Trolls were in the groups. For every twelve goblins, there was a hobgoblin. For every thirty goblins was a troll in the center. This was not going to be good. Paine's plan better work because fighting one troll was tough for three of us back in the day.

The goblins raised their flags into the air. The flag was once red but were now covered in human blood. This was a sign they desired war. Paine realized that he needed more time. His blood was pouring out and his heart was racing. The pressure to get this done was dwindling.

Paine had to wait until the goblins showed up first. This couldn't be premade since he would have to hold it up for a long time until the goblins actually showed up. The chances of his survival would be worse. All he had to do was have Michael keep the goblins a bay until the goblins dropped their flag and charged.

Paine stopped stabbing himself for a second. He opened the Void Storage. He opened it wide enough for a large beast to come out. A chimera slowly walked out and strutted it's stuff. The chimera was enormous. The soldiers were afraid that the chimera would try to destroy the wall.

Paine yelled, "Rufus! Go get your Supper!"

The chimera ran at the goblins. Fresh goblin meat was a delicacy for the chimera. Something about the taste of their blood would put the chimera into a frenzy. The lions head would eat most of them. I believe it was because their blood was flammable and the lion side would blow fire.

Paine didn't ask the question as to why the chimera loved eating goblins. He just knew that the chimera would kill a lot of them without question. Paine had splatter blood on the chimera. He gave it Barrier and watched the madness.

Did he name the chimera Rufus? He really was an animal lover at heart. He told me once that the Void Storage had zombies in it. I wondered if he named all of them as well. I do know he named the dragon Deathstroke. I kind of wonder if I will see him out here soon. The only time I saw him was when he ate Martin.

The chimera ran into the group of goblins like a dog chasing a car. It froze everything to the left and cooked everything to the right. The tail had a snake's body and was spitting poison a the goblin them eating them with the lion's head.

Michael saw the chimera was getting a lot of attention. He put on his Hell Armor and glowed bright purple. Lighting was surrounding him as he formed his swords in both hands. This was going to be his time to shine. He ran straight at the goblin horde and all you saw was heads pop off into the air. Bodies were flying everywhere. Blood and flesh were getting tossed in all directions. I could see a huge chunks of each dead goblins flying looking like a the air was now blood spray.

The Purple lightning around Michael was stunning the horde as they were all trying to catch him. I couldn't see his body. Michael was moving at superhuman speeds. My scan wasn't even good enough to see him.

Michael was definitely better than that day in the dungeon. The decapitations of the trolls were nothing to him. There were several trolls killed in less than a second. Michael might be able to destroy the horde all by himself at this rate.

Matilda was floating through the air allowing the lightning in the sky to strike down goblin after goblin. She kept cackling like a witch as it echoed through the kingdom.

The wyverns were closing into the walls. The archers were shooting off arrows. There were so many arrows that it blacked out the sun completely.

Matilda was striking them from the sky when the wyvern got close enough. She was having a hard time killing all them. Matilda was only able to strike one down at a time. The ones she did strike were losing control and dive bombing into the wall. The momentum was so bad that it splattered there blood and organs on the wall. The blood dripped down the wall, but the guts were sticking.

Chavez yelled, "Hell Cyclone!"

To the left side of the goblin hordes, a tornado filled with fire was tossing the goblins into the air and turning them into a crisp. The Fire Cyclone was following the goblins around and sucking them in incinerating them in large groups. The horde was not able to get close to us. They were afraid of being chase down by Chavez's move.

Chavez was laughing as he was taking large groups out. He was sweating hard as if the fire was right next to him. Chavez's clothes had so much sweat that it looked like Onyx drenched him in water.

Paine was still drawing blood from his chest. His wounds were healing so fast that he had a hard time stabbing himself fast enough to drain enough blood out of his body. Paine was using the skill Blood Ritual to work it around the city, but the blood wasn't moving fast enough.

King Augustus was standing there watching the monsters. Michael didn't care. He took on the horde by himself. I could see his body make weird gestures making fun of the goblins. Michael gave one a Wet Willie so hard that it's head exploded. The boy was insane, but I loved him for it.

Augustus said, "Is this all you got Goblin King? You're going to need to up your game if you want to win."

I decided to not hold back any longer. I shot off twenty arrows into the air. The arrow flew at the goblins allowing me to use my Star Spark and head shotting one after another. The numbers were greater than I anticipated. Seeing eighteen million goblins was quite a sight. You could not see an ounce of land for miles.

My arrows flew around striking all the little goblins. I was afraid at this distance the arrows would hit a troll and bounce off like before. I was doing my best, but this wasn't where I truly shined. Paine told us to stay on the wall. David seems to know the plan is mostly just standing there doing nothing at all.

Matilda stopped focusing on the center gate and floated toward the center of town. The wall was being surrounded. She was striking goblins and keeping them at bay. The sand melted and turned into sharp pieces of glass when cooled. That couldn't be good for the goblins as most of them were barefoot.

Onyx was casting a spell under the feet of trolls. Their feet were stuck and unable to move. The heat from the desert was melting it, but that was all the time she needed. The skin around her was turning a blue color. Everyone around her gave her room.

Onyx yelled, "Crystalized Spike!"

A giant piece of ice came out of the ground and froze those closest to it. The ones not closest to the source were stabbed with projectible pieces of ice that flew off the ice mountain. The goblins were trying to find a way through. There wasn't any room for error on their part. We kept casting and protecting the gate. At this rate, victory was at hand.

Darwin opened up a portal with a white room. It looked like he wasn't just making weapons anymore. He had a whole shop filled with toys. Darwin walked inside and closed the portal. I thought he was going to help, but it looked like he was just hiding. If he was going to hide, I should have told him to put Megan inside.

Loraine was putting down Mana Wells for the group. With the amount of magic everyone was using, we surely needed it. People around us were running low on mana. The fight was feeling never-ending as we tried to keep the horde at a distance.

Paine slit his throat to bleed for his ritual. He had a smile on his face as he was cutting himself. Paine truly was sick in the head. Paine would claim that every time he was stabbed a happy thought would automatically come into his head. I often wondered why were friends with these people.

Michael came back to Paine. Michael removed his helmet. He had an ill look on his face and began to throw up. I never saw him do that before. Paine didn't either. The Overdrive is natural, but it doesn't mean that there are no effects. He was feeling what we felt from the Overdrive when he carried us. This wasn't a good sign as there were still millions of goblins to go.

Michael ran back and pulled the dead bodies from the field in front of the gate. He was making a secondary wall around Paine and the gate with the bodies. The wall started small, but the corpses kept piling up around Paine. The goblins would have to climb over the bodies to get to him giving him more time.

Paine yelled, "You doing good."

Michael stopped for a second and said, "I can do this all day."

Michael sped in the direction of the most goblins. The decapitated bodies flew through the air like a bowling ball hitting pins. The sands were covered in so much green blood that you couldn't see the sands in the cleared-out spots.

I had my arrows come back to me. They were covered in green blood and wasn't sure if I wanted to even reuse them. The pungent smell was enough to make me want to throw up. The blood and brain matter was enough to make anyone call the arrows trashed. I stuck them in my quiver just in case, but I wasn't happy about it.

I pulled by my bow and charged it with a Fire Arrow. The fire elements surrounded me. There was a group of goblins flying on wyvern that Michael kept missing because he was focused on what was straight ahead.

Rufus, the chimera was a tough bitch. Paine called the chimera a boy's name, but it was female. I could see it from all the way here. The idiot didn't know how to gender his own pet.

David, Augustus, and Solomon all stood over the gate. The only one holding a weapon was Augustus. I wasn't sure why they were just watching. Solomon was clearly some sort of mage. Augustus should be out there fighting the goblins face to face. I don't know what David does, but Paine seems to insist he is a strong fighter.

Onyx was running out of mana from all the ice attacks. The heroes in the city were on the walls waiting to be told what to do. The mages were firing off spells to hold the goblins back. The archers were beginning to run out of arrows. The townspeople were making arrows and carrying them up to each post.

This was a nightmare and all Paine was doing was bleeding all over the damn ground. I thought this was going to be a great plan, but I haven't seen him begin to charge a single attack at them.

I shot Fire Arrow at the groups. The explosions coming from the shots were flying the goblins through the air. I hit a few trolls with it, but it just singed them a bit. The goblins brought a new pet to the raid. It was an Oliphant.

An Oliphant was a beast with four tusks. The nose on it stretched out twelve feet and large floppy ears. It looked a lot like an elephant, but it had large dragon-like wings on its back. The height of one was close to seven hundred feet. If that thing runs into the walls, we might be fucked. The only chance I had was to taking one down was to set the damn things on fire.

I shot off some Fire Arrows so that they would stick to the Oliphants and burn. I needed to use all my spirit to fire them off. I shot off the Fire Arrow. It was a direct hit. The Oliphant was flying into the air trying to blow the flames out. My flames were too strong to be taken out that easily. The flesh was burning on the Oliphant. You could hear it's sweet screams in the distance. That put a smile on my face.

Paine yelled up, "Is everyone within the city?"

Augustus exclaimed, "Yeah, do your magic!"

Paine cried out, "Barrier!"

The blood he put on the ground was forming a large barrier over the city. It came shooting over us. The barrier managed to reach thousands of feet into the air. The blinding white light from it was forming. The barrier was only five feet over the highest point of the castle. When the barrier fully connected, it sent a shockwave across the city that knocked weaker folks on there asses.

Michael and Paine were stuck outside the barrier. Everyone in the barrier was getting stocked up. This was his masterful plan to give us time to replenish. We didn't even get the chance to take out a million of them yet. This was not looking good as the goblins saw this as a chance to charge the barrier.

Michael came back to Paine and asked, "Now what?"

Paine said, "Defend me."

Paine placed his right hand on his armor and his left on the shield. He was giving the shield every little piece of mana that he had. To hold a shield that size from that many creatures would take a fucking miracle.

Paine screamed as he charged the barrier. He had a smile on his face as the pain had to be severe. Paine's eyes got wider and the barrier got brighter. People were filing up on arrows and visiting the closest Mana Well.

The Oliphants were flying into the air and charging the barrier. Each hit could be seen, heard, and felt. The barrier was holding, but for how long. This was nuts. The hobgoblins were smiling as they charged the barrier ready to completely destroy it.

I thought the barrier would be weakening, but with each hit it felt like it was getting stronger. Michael was slicing Paine's back every few seconds and tossing all enemies away. He sliced them in half and tossed their corpse into the air.

Michael stopped for a moment and looked up at me. He had tears in his eyes. I don't know what was about to happen but it was like he knew death was coming. Michael smiled up at me. I wasn't sure why, but he looked down.

Michael ran off and stacked the bodies around the gate. He made it so the bodies were as tall as half the wall. Blood was being soaked by the sand. I couldn't see Michael anymore. I saw his footsteps in the sand as it was being tossed everywhere.

Rufus did well, but five Oliphants surrounded Rufus and stabbed him with their tusks. Rufus dropped down but killed the five Oliphants with fire and poison. It was severely weakened and wasn't able to get back up. The trolls surrounded Rufus and beat him mercilessly until he didn't move anymore.

Paine was on the ground and felt his friend leave this world. He had an extra sight that none of us realized for a long time. Paine was able to see things in this world and the Void. I could see him crying at the loss of his beloved pet. It was the first death of the war.

Paine screamed and went into overdrive charging the shield even harder. I could see him running out of mana holding the shield was taking a major toll on him. There had to be millions of goblins and other beasts hitting the barrier.

Wyvern were attacking from the top and the only safe place was at the gate. The city was about to be overtaken. I can't believe we lost this badly. My heart was breaking as I looked behind me and saw all the children in the streets watching us fight for the city's future.

Paine yelled, " RAY OF LIGHT!"

Michael was standing next to him and said, "It was nice knowing you."

Paine said, "Fly you fool."

At that moment, Michael flew into the air seeing how far he could get. I could see the tinkle of the purple lightning. How far would he need to get to survive? Ray of Light was what Lucas used on Marcy. Is he really going to have the shield explode?

I yelled, "Everyone get into cover!"

A light shined across the land. I had never seen anything like this before. The light touched the land and incinerated everything in its path. Everything that was within six miles was now incinerated. The sand was a giant sheet of reflective glass.

The explosion was a thousand times worse than any nuke. I had no idea Paine had this kind of power. I couldn't see either of them. I could only think that they were both dead.

Michael was a demon and allergic to holy power. I could not see any form of life in front of the gate. Everyone was cheering as they all acknowledged that the threats were destroyed, but at what cost.

Chapter 11

Loraine ran over to David and said, "Find him. He has to be alive. Nothing can kill him. That is his whole thing."

Augustus grabbed her by the shoulders and said, "Calm down. If David finds him we will grab him. The sands are filled with glass and a search party is not possible. Only the strong can locate him. David do you feel his presence."

David replied, "I sense his body, but right now I don't sense a heartbeat."

I jumped off the wall into the city. I said, "Open the gate."

The guard said, "The king has instructed us to...."

I replied, "Unless you want me want me to stick my foot so far up your ass you'll be spitting toenails for a week. I suggest you listen to me."

The guard looked up and saw King Augustus nod to let the gate open to find our friend. I ran out the gate and stepped on the sand. The glassy sand was cracking under my weight. I saw my own reflection on the ground. There seemed to be no sign of Paine. I had a hard time seeing my friend.

I had Scan on and saw a warm signature. The image looked large like it might be him, but could be a goblin that survived. I just needed signs of movement to help me located Paine's position.

I had a hard time seeing through all the warm goblin blood. The blood was warming from the desert heat. The heat was beating down on me and messing with my Scan ability. I was seeing red wavy lines.

I took small steps through the glass shards. The shards were crunching under my weight. I was doing my best to not to cut my feet. It wasn't an easy feat. No pun intended.

I was positive that Paine was located. I had to lift up a large shard of glass from the location. The shard was heavy, but as a hero. I managed to toss it into the distance like a Frisbee.

The sand felt soft through my fingers. I knelt down and began to dig. The sand was flying through the air and bits of glass were still in it. I kept cutting my hands while digging and mixed my into the sand.

I saw a human hand in the sand. I finally got to him. My hand reached in and began to pull him out. It was like a man who fell into a frozen lake. I pulled on him and realized that my strength wasn't enough to yank him out.

I started digging Paine out some more I need to at least get to his head. I did my best to dig him out. I couldn't hear any breathing or feel any mana coming from him. This wasn't good.

My hands dug until I finally saw Paine's head. I grabbed his chin and pulled him out of the sand until his underarms appeared. His body was still functioning, but barely. I grabbed under Paine's right armpit and pulled him out. His body was placed on the glass surface to the left of us.

I opened Paine's mouth and sand was inside. The immortal had a weakness. It was mana. He never told anyone what his weaknesses were. Paine would just say that he had two weaknesses. I managed to figure out the mana thing all on my own.

I used my fingers and dug out most of the sand in his mouth. I felt so gross as the sand was cutting the inside of his mouth. The scraping was making a scratching sound. The blood was washing some of the sand down his throat.

As Paine's mouth was being cleaned out. A large object fell from the sky about thirty feet away. It hit the ground and glass flew everywhere. I covered my eyes and face.

A large piece of glass flew and stabbed me in the back. I reached back with my right arm barely able to touch the shard. I slowly pulled on it while wincing from the pain. I was having a hard time breathing. I thought the shard might have punctured my lung. I managed to pull it out. The healing was going to take a while. I was bleeding badly enough that the sand changed from green to red and orange.

I dragged Paine into the city. The guards grabbed his body when I got close enough. His body didn't seem to heal like it usually does. That sick masochist tried to actually kill himself.

The glass settled a bit as the wind was picking up the debris. The debris was slicing my skins and drawing out drops of blood. I didn't let the debris deter me.

The drop from the sky had to be Michael. All I could do was pray that he didn't die.

My feet went out into the glass ridden area. I knew object from the sky had to be Michael. As I got closer, my hopes were true. The object looked like Michael. He fell from the sky and left a crater in the ground. I had to wonder how high he was because the hole he made was at least six feet deep.

I ran out to see him. Glass from the wind was piercing his back. The bottoms of my feet were bloody from the shards. I didn't care. I saw him still breathing but was knocked out.

My mind took over. I wasn't going to let the pain prevent me from saving my love. Even if he was an ass. I got the strength to lift him up. I threw him over my right shoulder. My feet ran his body as fast as I could into the city. The gate was closed immediately.

Paine was already brought up the castle wall. I walked Michael up the steps to the wall hoping that I could find a healer that wasn't holy. His body was placed with his front facing the floor. I was pulling the glass shards from his back.

Matilda came down from the sky and stopped being a weather witch for a moment. Her mana was getting low and needed to drink from the Mana Well. Loraine ran over and was about to heal him with holy magic.

My hand was put out to stop her. I shook my head no. She wasn't even thinking about it. When she realized that harm would only come from it. Loraine backed away. Her heart was sinking and just focused on Paine.

Paine's eyes were opening. He choked for a moment and spit out sand. It blew like dust in the wind. He wanted to move, but his body wasn't letting him yet. It was crying out for more mana.

Michael just lie there suffering. He was trying to breathe. Purple blood was coming out of his mouth. David was coming over to find out what was going on. Why wasn't someone healing him? The wounds were deep. Michael was getting his power back. The wounds were closing very slowly. If he didn't pick up the pace, he would surely bleed to death.

David realized when he saw the purple blood. That was the blood of a demon. Michael wasn't a human after all. His heart seemed to be with the humans so not a word was said.

David cried out. "I need a Mistweaver Monk. This man needs attention."

A man ran to his aid. Mistweaver Monks were rare. The city was paying good money for all kinds of healers lately. The missions were getting hard and needed them for the local dungeons.

I could hear loud crunching from the distance. It couldn't be. They were all wiped out I thought. The wyvern riders were coming this way as over a million came this way. The group was going to be insane to kill. The glass on the ground wasn't even phasing them. Their green blood was spreading across the desert once again.

I want to believe that we will fight and win, but I'm not sure how without Michael and Paine. This had to end and fast. I held my bow upward and made a Fire Arrow. The arrow was being charged with everything I had. When this arrow goes off, I wanted to be noticed. The heat from the arrow was making me sweat hard.

I let loose of the arrow. It fired into the ground and made a big explosion killing over fifty of them. I felt my heart racing. That wasn't enough to save the day. I looked down at Sylvia and Diego. They seemed to know what to do.

The goblins had towers that they were pushing toward the wall. It looked like a giant rectangular box that stood upwards on wheels. The wheels were made of wood The tower was made of bamboo. The goblins rolled these across the glass only to get over the wall.

Wyvern were flying in closely. One swooped in and picked up one of the archers that was shooting at him. A wyvern took its long mouth scooped up an archer. It held the archer there only few seconds. The wyvern slowly chewed on him until he died. Blood was leaking out its jowls. This wasn't a good start.

I used Instant Teleportation to get right behind the goblin sitting on top the wyvern that just ate. He never saw me coming. I took out my daggers and sliced his throat from behind. The goblin was holding his neck as he was bleeding only to fall off the wyvern.

The wyvern didn't like me being on its back. It tried to snap at me while flying faster. I looked down. Holy shit, this was far up . My stomach felt like it was dropping to my feet. All I knew was that I needed to find a safe way down to the ground.

I waited until I got closer to another wyvern rider and stabbed the current wyvern with both daggers three times. The wyvern started to fall and ported over to the next one. I was in front of goblin on this one. The wyvern felt me on his back and tried to bite my head off. He missed and bit the head off of the goblin. I would call that a success.

I stabbed the back of the wyvern until it wasn't able to fly any longer. I fell from the sky. I knew this was not going to be my day. I saw another flying toward the castle and teleported over to it. I drove my right knife up into the goblin's skull. The goblins head was gargling as the knife was twisted.

My left knife swung around and sliced the wyvern's right wing. The dead goblin was thrown off as it tilted to the wyverns right. My legs straddled the wyvern to stay on. I stabbed the wyvern repeatedly until there was enough blood dripping to drown a whimpering goblin.

The wyvern tried to land itself, but instead flew directly into the wall. I tried to hold on for dear life. The impact killed the wyvern. There was wyvern blood and guts sliding down the wall. I should have died from the impact. I managed to stay alive. My body was plastered onto the wall leaving a huge indent. I was stuck there.

I hit the wall hard and stuck the knives into the cracks. This was the only reason I was able to stay on the wall. David used some sort of invisible force to bring me to the top of the wall. I took out three wyverns. That made me feel fantastic.

I looked into the sky and howled. I was having the time of my life. I looked around and saw mages and archers shooting everything they had at the enemy.

I began to feel shame. My powers only killed three goblins and wyvern. These people were giving it theire all and killing so much more. I didn't have time to gloat. The problem was that my stamina wasn't good at the moment because I used to much spirit force to teleport all over the battlefield. I was really tired.

Chavez closed his eyes and called out a Fire Wall. A Fire Wall is a simple fire spell that brings flame up from the ground. It creates a wall that holds back weaker monsters since it would incinerate them. The heat was immense and could be felt from the top of the wall. The Fire Wall wrapped around the half the castle wall. The only way for a goblin to get by was to go around.

Chavez's eyes turned bright orange. I could see the sweat dripping down his brow. His tears turned to fire as he was pushing himself to the brink. His clothes were burning. His robes were burnt to ash, but luckily his pants were still intact.

Michael was slowly healing. The holy energy was beginning to wear off. He was still in severe pain. After some time, his demon side was coming back and healing him. The monk managed to close his wounds but didn't bring him back to his full potential.

Loraine stopped healing Paine for a moment. Loraine said, "Sit down! Look at yourself."

I really was a mess. My clothes were torn. I was bleeding to death from the glass. I breathed in enough glass debris that I was puking up blood. This might have been part of the reason I was feeling so tired.

Loraine put her hands on me. I could feel a warm feeling that combatting the cold from the wind. My body was closing up the holes and spitting out the glass shards. I had and entire shattered window pop out of my body. I felt so refreshed. My right hand wiped the blood away that was on my forehead. I was ready for a another round. Loraine pointed for me to sit there and rest.

Paine just laid there next to me drinking from the Mana Well as Loraine babied him. She propped up his head on her lap and poured the water into his mouth. Paine kept going in and out of consciousness. He had a smile on his face like there was a good dream that he never wanted to let go. The guy was weird.

Augustus, Solomon, and David slide on leather boots. The boots looked like the ones from the old world. It had rubber bottoms and shoe laces. It was clear they had a Creationist on hand who remembered the old world. I wonder what kind of goodies Darwin will give us. I kind of just wanted running water with a proper bathroom.

Augustus, Solomon, and David jumped off the wall to the ground. The glass wasn't affecting their feet, but instead crushed it. Chavez opened the wall and let them pass closing it behind them. The goblin hit the ground and tried to appear scary. It didn't work as the royals stayed in power for a reason. In a battle, they are all savages.

Solomon began to glow. His body was changing shape and looked like he was becoming two-dimensional. Solomon looked out at the goblins and pointed as his skin turned black. The stars in the sky were forming it looked like his body changed. His whole body turned into a Void Storage portal. He was like Paine.

Solomon shot off lines of Void magic. He was able to take out entire crowds of goblins with each shot piercing through their bodies. The move reacted like a Void Sphere and sliced the goblins in half. It made me wonder if Paine was holding back and he was able to be like this.

David pushed the goblins back and slowly walked forward. He launched eat goblin into the air and clenched his fist. With every clenched fist, a goblin's body was smashed like it was in the palm of his hand. He pushed with his right and crushed with his left. There was nothing around to indicate that he was using power except his motions. The man was clearly a hard man to kill.

Augustus was a Barbarian and charged into the goblins. He leaped into the air and dropped down in the middle of a group. The ground rose up as if gravity was pulling them in all directions ripping off their limbs and caving in their bodies. Augustus swung his axe around in a circle. The axe was pulling in every enemy around them. Even the hobgoblins that were three times the size of normal goblin were being ripped apart by Augustus's gravitational pull.

Every moment they spent out there was dwindling the numbers. Augustus was able to heal fast like Marcy. His power was increasing with each blow. The difference seemed to be his aura was black and Marcy's was red.

A troll charged Augustus and tried to slam its club on him. Augustus stood his ground and held his axe up in the air. He blocked the blow and pushed upward knocking the troll off his feet. Augustus ran up the troll's left leg and bounced off its stomach. He swung the axe around and decapitated the troll.

The goblins were striking Augustus, but he hit a point of rage that did no damage to him at all. He swung the axe over and over again killing every goblin in this sight. The green blood was covering his whole body making him go into an unstoppable frenzy.

Goblins ran over and attacked Solomon. His body was still in the weird Void form that looked like stars in his body. Every time a goblin hit him the weapon or limbs would disappear. A goblin punched him and all that was left was a bloody stump where the hand used to be. Solomon was shooting from a distance and walking toward the goblins making their bodies fall apart.

David stopped for a moment and sat down. He was trying to focus on the crowds around him. His aura was changing shape and groups of enemies were getting squashed. It was square so it looked like a telekinetic fly swatter dropped on them and squashed the goblins to death.

The warriors on the wall were jumping down and charging the goblins. The mages attacked from a distance with everything they had. I had no idea why there were this many heroes in the middle of the desert. It was like the city brought outsiders and we were the final ones to show up.

The goblins attacked and tried to break through. The warriors held their ground and didn't budge an inch. The paladins were using their shields to block the attacks and followed up with judgments. The wall was their priority. The trolls tried to grab the paladins, but they moved too fast.

The charged barrier might have just won us this battle. The people I felt were farmers were actually heroes with vast powers. Diego and Sylvia were waiting for my instructions. They were my last resort. I was afraid of them getting injured or dying. I cared for them more than the king.

The king and his brothers decided to fall back. Their energy was depleting and couldn't fight for much longer. Solomon was the first to go back to the castle. He flew through the air and got back to his spot above the gate. Solomon turned off his Void Form. He dropped to his knees and tried to catch his breath. Solomon was almost completely out of mana.

David tried to hold his ground. Blood was dripping out of his nose. He kept pushing the enemy back. While he still could, David flew back up to the spot above the gate. It was a good effort on his part.

Augustus was the last to leave. The horde was surrounding him. He looked at David and held up his arms. David used a telekinetic ability to pull his brother into the air and put him at the gate wall. Chavez lowered his flames for a moment so that it was easier to bring him back.

The gate now was just being defended by Chavez's Fire Wall. A bunch of the goblins ran at the wall trying to drain Chavez's power so the trolls could get in unscathed. Each goblin was turned into a crispy corpse on the ground. The smell of the burning flesh was horrific.

Diego looked back at me and said, "We aren't babies let us loose. It's time."

I was really hesitant, but I had no choice. Sylvia was scratching her neck and waiting for the go-ahead. This was going to take a lot out of me. I knew it had to be done. I put my hands on the wall. My hands held on for dear life. This was going to suck.

On the left side of my body, I was turning red and glowing. On my right side, I was turning blue and glowing. My skin was peeling and it looked like colorful lightning bolts going up my arms and through my body.

I said," Get them. PREDATOR!"

Diego and Sylvia jumped off the edge. Sylvia's fur was glowing red. Diego's fur was glowing blue. I could hear their laughing as they charged into the horde of monsters. The goblins didn't seem afraid at all. Predator only made them three times their normal size. I couldn't wait until they realized what was really coming.

They both charged hard and the king looked at me as if I just slaughtered my animals. I was wincing in pain as this was the first time I ever tried this. I thought letting their little waves of laughter howl and echo causing the goblins their true dread. Chavez let them through the flames for only a moment. He had trust in me.

I cried out, "KAIJU!"

My hyenas grew up. I'm not talking a little grown-up. They were over three thousand feet in size. Their tails were strong enough to break down the wall on their own. The glow off them was so strong it blinded the goblins. Even at that great distance, the people on the wall were blinded as well.

I smiled as I saw my babies finally grow into fierce monsters of their own. They were carnivores and very hungry. I saw them bite down and eat trolls whole. They would attack with their tails dropping down onto the goblins. If it didn't kill them. It would destroy and paralyze them at least.

My teeth glowed blue and red fighting against these monsters. I was using a hive mind. I loaned the hyenas my strength just like the goblins. I was wondering how long I could keep this up as my body felt like it was broken. Loraine ran over to me and started to heal me as she heard my bones breaking.

I wasn't giving up. A priest came over to me and gave me a personal blessing. Another priest gave me Mana Restoration. Mana Restoration is a hardcore transfer system that has a priest give their personal mana to a hero. The difference between Mana Well and Mana Restoration is that Mana Well is a slow mana recovery system that helps a person build their own mana source. Mana Restoration is a direct flow of mana put into your body and being siphoned by the healer. With all three of these priests, I wasn't planning on giving up anytime soon.

I struggled to keep it up as Diego and Sylvia were the only ones protecting the gate now. My muscles were bulging out and my clothes were tearing worse. I wasn't even paying attention as my breasts were getting bigger and starting to pop out.

Kaiju took total concentration as they hit, bit, and scratched their way through the horde. I would say my kill count was hitting in the millions at this point. I couldn't tell as my hair was changing color and blinding me from what was truly going on. I went from blue to red.

I, eventually, went completely blind only seeing blue on my right side and red on the other. How many of these damn goblins were there. I lost control and my babies began to shrink. I had them out there for fifteen minutes wreaking havoc. I just couldn't hold it anymore. I started to vomit blood. I collapsed for a moment. My body was crackling under the pressure.

Diego and Sylvia noticed the height difference and ran to the wall. They got to the wall and waited to be hoisted up. David used his telekinesis and pulled both of them onto the wall. This was not good. There had to be a million more at least. Everyone had used up all their mana.

Paine got up and walked to the wall. He regained most of his mana back. That guy was not going down without a fight. He killed over ten million goblins and trolls on his own. He wasn't going to let us down. He could barely stand but was eager to fight again.

Michael got up despite the fact that he was still wounded. He stood over at the edge of the wall next to Paine. His skin was changing. There were red scales and the horns were coming in.

Paine said, "You got control."

Michael's demon teeth came in and said, "Fuck control. Let's have some fun."

Michael's wing grew out and he flew down to the goblins. The goblins charged at him bringing their towers to scale the wall. Michael destroyed most of the towers in seconds. He was smart enough not to let the goblins get any kind of advantage if he would help it. His speed was a lot slower in this form. His body was clearly stronger and had higher defenses. Michael took on every hit he could. The attacks didn't even phase him because of his demon skin. The swords came out and swung them around slicing everything in sight laughing hard.

Michael sped up and killed everything in front of him. He missed three towers. The towers worked their way around the wall of flames Chavez had up.

The goblins got the towers to the wall. Chavez was trying to light them on fire. He was so tired that he didn't have the strength to strike them down. There were too many. I wanted to do something like use Fire Arrow, but my spirit was drained to much. Something needed to happen and quick.

A portal to a white room opened up. Darwin walked out with a minigun and a smile on his face. You know like in the old world. It had a spiral barrel with six barrels. There was a piece on the end that looked like a fighter plane steer thing and a large belt with enough ammo to blow a hole in the castle.

Darwin yelled, "Sorry I'm late for the party! DUCK!"

Darwin fired that gun using every round he had. The castle was being ripped apart as he aimed it wherever there was a goblin. The towers were being shredded to pieces. Goblins were being shot up and tossed from the towers. Their bodies would hit the ground and explode. The goblins limbs were flying with the gut blood sinking into the sand. Darwin's ways were definitely reckless, but everyone loved him for it.

Darwin didn't stop there. Once the top area around us looked secure. He pointed it down range at the goblins and fired away. There was no stopping him as millions of bullets were firing and their hot casings were flying everywhere. I believe he was trying to show off and save the day.

The goblins were dwindling as both Darwin and Michael were slaughtering the last million. I believed we were going to win this as long as someone was able to fight the good fight.

Michael was killing left and right. He had a smile on this face enjoying his work. The monsters were fleeing toward him. Something in the back was attacking the goblins.

There appeared to be an even greater threat than Michael. All the goblins were running towards Michael. When they realized that Michael wasn't going to be defeated. Every goblin around the castle stopped and ran to attack him..

I couldn't figure out why, but the hive mind felt Michael was too much of a threat and tried to take him out. He was making high pitched noises that might be drawing in the goblins.

Behind all the bodies was a mysterious figure. It was a paladin with an evil red aura that I never saw before. It was like Michael and this mysterious were drawn toward each other. They both had savagery on their face. The two of them were ready to fuck up anything that came into their path.

The bloodlust from both of them made me feel queasy. I knew that at the end of this battle, those two were going to end up fighting each other. Michael had his devilish grin as he looked over at the mysterious paladin.

Michael swung his swords faster and more violently killing each goblins and trolls to get to him. This was when Michael met his true rival in life.

Chapter 12

The mysterious paladin pulled out his sword and began to fight. The shield was on his left. The mysterious figure bashed each goblin and stabbed them. A troll thought he had the paladin and dropped a club onto him. The paladin stood his ground. He formed two red knives with his hands and jumped through the troll's chest. There was a giant gaping hole through its chest before it collapsed.

The paladin put the shield on his back and the sword in its sheath. His red daggered hands were slicing through the rear of the group making them only a mile away from each other. The paladin sliced and diced until goblins surrounded him. This didn't stop the mysterious stranger as he spun around. Blood and flesh were sticking to his armor. The goblin's blood was being soaked up by his daggers.

A hobgoblin ran over and grabbed the mysterious strangers head with his left hand. The paladin leaned down. He used the red hand dagger to swing upward and sliced open the hobgoblin's stomach. The paladin's helmet was ripped off. He looked our way. His face was missing and part of the back of his head disappeared. The paladin-looking thing had no jaw, parts of the muscle on its forehead, and no skin. The eyes looked like it was popping out of the skull or at least whatever was part of the skull.

The paladin raised its arms into the air and all the goblins were raised with it. I watched as all the goblins were having their blood sucked out of them. It was turning into a green ball over the paladin's head. The paladin swallowed the blood in two seconds.

The goblins kept running at him, but everything within a few feet of the paladin got the blood sucked out of it. The two oliphants that were left tried to jump him for a kill. They were superior beasts and thought stepping on him would finish the job. The paladin blocked the foot with his blades. He absorbed all its blood turning the oliphants into a shriveled husk.

Michael was on the other side slicing through them to get to the evil paladin. With all the blood going into the paladin's mouth, he grew a little piece of skin on the outside. There appeared to be no end as the paladin drained everything that got near him.

The closer the paladin got to Michael the wider the range was. He was now absorbing every goblin within twelve feet of him. The same went for Michael. His wings were growing, his swords were getting bigger, and all we could see were flashes of light as he was slaughtering everything getting close to the castle.

The paladin had formed a jaw after sixty thousand kills. His face was coming back slowly. It was like the paladin was meant to be there. The paladin had long teeth pop out the top of its mouth. I truly believed it was some sort of really strong vampire.

Michael jumped into the air and noticed that there were twelve wyvern riders coming for the castle. In less than a second, he slaughtered all of them. I couldn't tell if he was in control or not. He seemed to have a level head but killed indiscriminately. There was no focus on what to kill but wanted to let the new guy kill as many as possible. Michael didn't see the guy as a threat.

Michael stayed in the air and watched as the paladin destroyed everything around him. The goblins knew that if they didn't take us down there was no chance of winning the war. The goblins continued to run at the paladin. His hair was starting to grow out. It appeared to be either white or yellow. It was hard to tell from the wall. My scan was working in overdrive to see everything.

Diego and Sylvia were lying next to me as I watched everything over the wall. I saw Michael's black aura getting bigger with each step this paladin was taking toward us. This was going to end in a duel.

There were only a hundred goblins left and the face appeared to be fully filled out. I couldn't believe my eyes. Blonde hair, blue eyes, and a grin that made me want to cry. It was Lucas. He was alive, but something felt off. Michael was face to face with his old friend watching him kill the last of the goblins.

The sand had so many dead bodies on the ground, but he was leaving nothing but husks still after their deaths. These two were demons. My father knew they were both going to be demons. I wasn't sure how to handle it.

Michael came to the ground. He said, "I mourned your death hard. I will never mourn it again."

Lucas replied, "I was told not to kill the warlock. I was just to defend the home. I wasn't near strong enough then. I'm more than enough now. After four long years, It feels good to have my face back. I see you got a few tricks."

Michael responded, "You a demon."

Lucas said, "Yeah in a way. We just need a Death Knight and we got the trifecta. Maybe we only need one demon in this world?!"

Michael strengthened his swords. The people on the wall tried to watch and see the outcome of the fight. I could see Lucas and Michael about to kill one another. Maybe this time they won't destroy a city or town over their stupidity.

Lucas increased the range on his dagger hands. His eyes turned bright red and his teeth were gushing dry blood. Horns made of blood were pushing out of his cheeks and back toward his ears.

Michael increased his purple lightning around his body. Michael's eyes turned purple and the horns grew larger. He was learning control the demons inside of him. The demons fought him every step of the way. The demons wanted to escape.

Michael went into speed mode where he couldn't be seen. Lucas was swinging at him, but couldn't as Michael was hitting the armor. The armor appeared to be impenetrable. I can only imagine how much holy power was in it now.

Lucas said, "What lovely horns you have? Judgment!"

Lucas stabbed Michael in mid-hit. The thing about Michael was he was wild but predictable. If you caught the pattern, there was a way to take him down. Lucas remembered this from when he went on missions with us.

The purple blood was falling as Michael's weakness was holy energy. This was game over clearly. Michael just smiled as Lucas said, "Ray of Light!"

The sword glowed from the Ray of Light. He was about to blow Michael in half. Michael just smiled at Lucas and winked. The Judgment exploded and did nothing to Michael. What the hell was going on?

Michael laughed at Lucas in a deep sinister way. He stood there with his nose flared and his eyes wide. Michael's horns went back into his head. The scales were disappearing and the wings were working their way back into his shoulders. Michael was once again completely human.

Michael said, "Do you really think that puny holy magic has an effect on me? I'm half human after all. My defenses are enough, I have felt holy energy in my body for years. If you want to defeat me now, you will need new tricks."

Michael was right. He survived an explosion that wiped out half the goblin race at least. When holy magic worked on him, was only when he lost control. The holy magic was keeping the demons inside at bay now him personally. All he has to do is get the demons inside of him to stay out of a fight and he isn't weak to holy anymore.

This is going to sound strange, but he might be resistant to holy magic. For many years, he wore holy armor imbued with holy magic. High amounts of holy magic sparked him, but never truly hurt him. The whole time I thought it was in remembrance of his friend and hiding. Michael was just training up to gain resistance.

Lucas said, "I want to kill you. You let me die. You hid like a child. I don't want to hear the same crap that Draco told me. I don't want to hear that you were controlled by your demons and couldn't. We were supposed to be best friends and you buried me. Give me one good reason why I shouldn't kill you right now."

Michael had tears in his eyes. He walked over to Lucas and said, "Welcome home brother."

Lucas wanted to stab but was filled with emotion himself. He grabbed Michael back and held him closely. Both men were crying. It was gross. What kind of woman actually wants to witness two grown men cry? I know when I was in the first world. I wanted to watch men cry, but men are such ugly criers. I had to look away.

Darwin said, "I feel much better knowing I didn't have to use the nukes."

At first, I thought he was joking, but the man just pulled a minigun out of his storage portal. I have no idea what else he made over his sixty years in there. I was just hoping that he made some sort of awesome vehicle that would have us travel better. This walking everywhere shit is for the birds.

Lucas had to find his helmet now. With all the dead corpses on the ground, I think it would be tough. The bodies did become a problem as the next day the wyrms were coming around to eat them and we got stuck in the Zahn for over a month.

You would think that there would be some sort of a celebration for defending the city, but there wasn't. According to Augustus with animals grabbing over eighteen million in corpses and the payments to all the guild members that stepped up to help. Zahn couldn't afford a celebration

I asked Paine if he could pay for some of it and his response was. "I agree with Augustus. There is no reason to celebrate. We just need to get blessed and see how much we have grown."

The group got back to our room. Lucas ran off in a different direction. I think the king wanted him to explain himself. It wouldn't take much as all he would have to say is, I came from Tryanon and I'm a freaking prince.

I laid down in my bed staring at the ceiling. There wasn't a whole lot to do until the night came. There was a weird design on the boards. People were carving into them. There were names with hearts around them and blood-sealed promises. I wanted to do this with Michael. I wanted him to see me as an actual mate, but those words spoken before battle just pissed me off. "I know." What the hell was that supposed to mean?

Michael came over and sat on the bed next to me. I was mad still. I didn't even want to look at him. I turned over to my right and looked away. He wasn't getting the hint. I wanted to cry, but couldn't work up the tears.

Michael said, "I've been thinking since we were nine that you were Jamie. The truth is that my dreams seem to tell me a different story. I remembered who she was in a completely different context as we were partners with codewords to tell each other about kills. I have tested you numerous times over the years to see if you were her, but you failed all of them until one day I straight up asked. You denied to be her. You know me though. So I am deeply confused."

I didn't want to discuss this with him. Not right now. I was in really bad pain from doing Kaiju for so long. Hell, I saved the day to a certain extent. My powerful moves probably leveled up a lot. The downside was that the effects on my body were worse than my worst period.

Michael continued, "You began to love me the moment you saw me. I just can't remember who would since Jamie was the only person in my life that showed me any affection or gave a damn. I thought maybe a woman that I saved or a foster sister. I tried to put the pieces together, but none of it made sense. The only reason I brought up is that you claimed a hero saved your life and I dwelled on that for so long.

You died at the same age that Jamie was when I died. I thought so hard that you were her. Can you release me from this agony? Can you tell me who you are?"

I turned around and yelled, "What does it matter who I used to be? I'm lying here in pain trying to make the best of things. I don't want to move and you are trying to talk to me. I just wanted you to see me for who I am. I have thought many times if I should tell you who I was. The truth is. You knowing who I am won't make any difference. You love my sister Matilda anyway.

Matilda is awful toward you. You seem drawn to her instead so go off and love her instead. I don't care. I tried to tell you that I loved you before we went into battle. You said, "I know" which is a really shitty thing to do. What if you actually died out there? Your last words to me were "I know." All you think about is yourself. I should just beat you with a blue umbrella. Maybe that would knock some sense into you."

Michael said, "Blue umbrella. That is oddly specific. In my dreams, there was a young girl with her mom. The mom had a blue umbrella, but I didn't see a woman like that fawning over me. I saved you didn't I."

I said, "Shut up."

Michael responded, "I knew that I just needed one more piece. Time works differently in the Void. You were that little girl I saved. Your reaction to what I told you about my life makes sense now. I didn't want people putting pieces together on me. About what kind of person I was. I was a murderer and killed so many people with the help of Jamie. That's why I hoped you were her, but you aren't are you."

I said, "It doesn't matter. You want your precious Jamie anyway. Knowing my luck. Matilda is Jamie and I never stood a chance."

Michael walked over to my bed and rubbed my right shoulder. He was hurting me, but I didn't say a word since he was trying. I could feel my eyes starting to water. Why did I bring up the umbrella? Did I really want him to know that badly?

Michael took off his shirt and crawled into bed with me. His purple hair was beautiful in its own way. His body was sweaty and badly bruised still from when Lucas put Judgment on him. He laid there and held me as close as he could. I felt warm and loved for the first time in a long time.

I wrapped my arms around him and said, "You know I don't actually love you right."

Michael laughed and said, "Sure you don't. I wouldn't have it any other way."

Michael was so warm and gentle as can be. A demon should not make you feel this way. His sweat smelled like cotton candy. Everything around him was arousing like a pheromone that draws you like a trap.

I looked up at Michael. He held me by the back of my ears. I don't know why, but every time he does this I feel horny. My ugly ass ears betrayed me again. Their sensitive nature made me squirm. He gazed into my eyes. The pupils in his eyes moved around in a circle like he was trying to hypnotize me. He finally manned up and went in for a kiss.

I tried to reject the kiss, but my body wanted more. He was gentle to the touch and instead of saying he loved me he was showing me the best way possible. I wasn't sure what to say after the kiss was done.

Michael got out of the bed and put on his shirt. He said, "It's sealed." and walked out the door.

I looked over at Loraine. She had a huge smile on her face. Her arms were up by her chest. Her arms were shaking in excitement. Loraine had this big smile on her face. She looked around to make sure nobody else was in the room.

Loraine said, "Tell me everything. What just happened and are you two a thing now?"

I said, "I don't know what we are."

Loraine replied, "That was a good kiss. I have never seen him look at Matilda the way he looked at you just now. What did you guys say?"

I closed my eyes and put my pillow over my face. I really didn't wish to talk about it, but I knew she wasn't going to let me go until I did. Loraine removed the pillow and looked at me bug-eyed. I was going to have to give her something or she will never leave me alone.

I said, "He figured out who I was in the last world. I was nothing special to him, but he was to me. I have watched his every move for the last six years. I feel like such a stalker sometimes."

Loraine smiled and began to heal me. She came up to heal me since everyone was talking about the Kaiju situation downstairs and how it hurt me.

Loraine held onto my right arm and a gold glow came over me. I was feeling better, but tired.

Loraine said, "You need anyone to talk to. I'm always around. I miss girl gossip. You might be the only girl in the group to gossip with."

I asked, "What were you in the old world?"

Loraine replied, "I was a Japanese pop singer."

Loraine walked out of the room and down with the others. I fell asleep as this was the first moment I could in a long time. The darkness worked its way in and I dreamed a little dream.

Chapter 13

I woke up and Megan was by my bedside staring at me. She was breathing heavily and had a smile on her face. She was cute, but not cute enough to be inches from my face when I woke up.

Megan said, "Guess what. I am three thousand two hundred and forty-seven years old today. I'm going to be nine soon."

I said, "Great, it's almost time for bed. I'm trying to rest."

I took a moment to realize that tonight was a new moon and I needed to do the math in my head. This girl didn't realize how many years that was. I don't think the slavers realized that she was already nine. The slavers tried to make her seem younger for pedophiliac reasons those sick bastards.

I got out of bed and said, " Would you like to try and get your blessing tonight? I would love to be the one to take you."

Megan said, "I'm not nine years old yet. I have to wait."

I said, "What if I told you your birthday was seven days ago?"

Megan seemed confused. She tried to count, but counting on her fingers wasn't working as the number was too high. I knew this was going to be a shock to most of us since they told us she was younger.

I walked down and saw Loraine drinking a pint at the table with Michael and Paine. I went over to the table and slammed my hands down. The table felt like it was about to snap in half.

I said, "Do you know how old Megan is?"

Paine said, "They told us she was eight years old. Why?"

I replied, "She is nine. The young girl just got done telling me how many days old she is. The girl kept count by days and nobody with a brain was around. Either that or the plan to sell her for sex acts was more appealing with the younger age."

Paine responded, "Well, how long has she been nine?"

I said, "Seven days."

Paine replied, "Well that is an easy mistake. Happy birthday, kiddo. A little on the late side, but happy nonetheless. Let's see if we can get you into the church tonight. This should be interesting to see if she is a priest or not. We planned on going anyway for ourselves."

Loraine looked at Megan and asked, "You ready to go sweetheart."

Megan scratched under her collar around her neck. I wish we could take it off her, but people might kidnap her for slavery. What a strange world we live in when being a slave might be safer than being free.

The group left out the door. I didn't see Matilda anywhere. Maybe she was already at the church. Onyx, Darwin, and Chavez were in a corner waiting for us to go. They followed us to the church as if it were a requirement.

The walk down the street was hot and needed some form of cooling down period. I'm not sure why, but the room we were staying in was cool and bearable. Maybe because it was on the top floor, but something was going on. I never wanted to leave now.

The road was covered in sand and stone. I was doing my best not to stub my toes on the rocks since they were hard to see. The shops were closed for the day since the war broke out, but tomorrow I'm sure they will be open again.

The wind was picking up and blinding my eyes. I will never get used to this much sand. I feel gross all day. The place was so bad that I felt the need for a bath three times a day. Every time my arms moved I felt a grinding in my armpits. You could hear it too. I was just hoping nobody could hear the sand in my vagina. I could definitely feel it, but the crunching would be completely unappealing.

The group finally made it to the church. There was a line. Everyone and their mother were trying to get blessed tonight. I guess everyone realized that they spiked in power after a large combat scenario and wanted to reap the rewards.

I used my Scan and saw the priests sitting and watching all the people. This was two nights in a row and their main job was to protect the site. I can see now why they have it set up for twice a month. This would drain anyone and the High Priest had to be there. There was no show this time. We just all had to be patient.

Megan was at the front of the group since we were all eager to see if she became a priestess tonight. She could have been wrong about the number of days. The line was bad enough that some of the people decided to hold off for another day. Since people now know they can do it any day. The priests might have to find a way to explain it away.

After about an hour, Megan got to go to the podium. The priests asked if the group wanted parchments. I asked for one. The truth was these priests were cool for a clergy. I didn't mind supporting them after yesterday. The parchments wouldn't have done anything for rest of us. We were too powerful to be properly read. Well except for the other slaves. Paine didn't want people to know things about them for a reason. He never explained to us what it was.

It was Megan's turn. She was so cute with her nervousness. I remembered my first blessing. I actually skipped up to the platform. The priests were so mad at me. The after-effects weren't pleasant, but was worth it in the end. Let's see how she reacts.

Megan went to the platform and gave the parchment to the High Priest. She had a smile on her face. The High Priest saw her slave collar and looked at Paine. Paine just smiled and nodded his head yes.

Megan was on her knees with her hands clasped together actually praying to God. Tears were coming down as it sounded like she was talking to someone. This was a good sign, but no light was coming down on here.

The weird part about her blessing was that the light came from inside her instead of the sky. It shot straight up into the sky. Her body was floating which was normal, but her hand reached out like she was waiting for an adult to hug her. Wings sprouted from her back and a golden light shined off her skin. Her hair turned a golden color and her eyes turned blue. She was now a naturally blonde asian girl. Which is weird in itself.

Megan gained some muscle on her from the process. It was like she was the polar opposite of Michael. Priests aren't melee types so this was very strange to me. Holy energy was flowing out of her mouth. The longer she was up there the more she blinded the people in the courtyard. The power felt like she was about to explode.

Megan floated to the ground and her eyes had a golden color with gold lightning traveling around them. She ran at Paine and jumped high waiting for him to catch her. Paine didn't hesitate to catch her.

Paine said, " I'm so proud of you. Did you forget something?"

Megan was happy with herself but forgot the parchment. She ran up to the platform and tried to get the parchment. The High Priest had it in his hand. The High Priest smiled at her.

The High Priest said, "Do you want to know what you are? I see you are a level 1. I think you'll be surprised that you're something special."

Megan nodded her head in excitement. We didn't have anything to worry about because we guessed Holy, Discipline, or Juggernaut Priest. The weird thing was she wasn't any of those. There was a fourth option that most of us forgot or didn't know about. I wish Matilda was here to help explain what this was.

The High Priest named off her stats. The intelligence and defense seemed high. The abilities were the part that mattered the most to us. How was she going to fit in with the group?

The High Priest said, "Your skills are as follows. Holy Breaker Passive to punch down any demon that comes your way. Penance Stare to make any adversary relive their nightmares and crimes until you stop it. The last skill is Holy Regeneration so that you can regenerate your mana and heal yourself. This is ongoing until you kill your last foe."

Paine looked confused and said, "I thought she was a priest. I am a paladin who lived in the church in Tryanon. How come I never heard of any of these skills."

The High Priest said, "She is a Priest. All three abilities are attached to the rare Titan Priest. They are destroyers of demons. You are a lucky man to have found this gem. She will make a great tank-like class for your group."

The group had him and Lucas for tanks. They didn't need another class, but having a holy class dedicated to destroying demons seemed like a good idea. She emitted so much healing power during her blessing that I wonder what her abilities do. We will have to read up on this.

Onyx, Chavez, and Darwin went next. Darwin was the most surprising since he was now a level hundred and thirty-seven. What the hell is going on with this guy? What has he been doing? I know he went ten years without a single blessing, but there has to be more than meets the eye. After he finished, he went right back into his garage portal.

I said, "Paine, he needs to be out here supporting the group."

Paine said, "Worry about yourself. I have a project that he is working on."

That was kind of rude. The guys are always keeping me in the dark about stuff. It was really pissing me off. I was just trying to help and...well I guess he is right. They aren't my slaves. I just wanted him to be part of the group.

I took my turn. Angela spoke to me yesterday so I didn't think this was going to take long. I walked up with Diego and Sylvia in my pocket. I am so glad that I figured out how to shrink them. It was horrible leaving them outside the town because they would cause damage and fear.

I raised my hands and floated into the air. I thought nothing of it at first until I felt a weird surge of energy. My eyes were turning red and my skin was bubbling. I closed my eyes waiting for it to end.

The air was calm. When I opened my eyes. I was in the Void. The place was dark. I mean there were no stars, forests, or even Angela. I stood up off the ground and walked forward. The Void still provided a little light from my steps.

Diego and Sylvia were missing this time. I believe they weren't able to return since they fused with the hyenas. My heart felt like it was about to pop out of my chest. This felt different for some reason.

A bright light shined from the sky, it was Angela. She smiled at me. I was waiting for her to speak, but she wasn't saying a word. Something must have happened. I saw her lips moving, but nothing was coming out.

I walked three steps forward to get closer and got hoisted into the air. The Void put me fifty feet into the air and left me floating. I felt like I had jumped out of an airplane. My stomach felt like it was left a million feet above me. My body began to glow.

Angela flew next to me and said, "Are you ready?"

I asked, "Ready for what?"

Angela flew forward at an intense speed. I saw streaks of light flying past me. Green lightning was following me. I didn't understand what was going on. How was I flying this time? Does this mean I would be able to fly now as an ability? I don't know of any hunters that can fly yet.

The two of us got faster and faster. We went up slightly and was a dimensional gateway to a well-lit world. I was guessing it to be Heaven as cheerful voices came from it. The place felt welcoming. The warmth of the light was pressing upon my body. The comfort and joy was overwhelming. I didn't wish to leave, but knew I had to. I needed to finish my job on Kepogle first.

I felt myself plummeting from the air as rainbows surrounded me. The rainbows twirled and smacked me hard. I was hurled back and forth. My body was losing control. I bounced off the rainbows like a pinball machine. My eyes were closed. I was hoping by closing my eyes it would send me to the second world. I wasn't sure how much abuse I could take before this ended.

I was within twenty feet of the ground. My body sped up and hit the ground hard. I don't know what purpose of that was. I felt pain and couldn't move. The pain reminded me of the time I was flung into the air in the desert. I could barely move, but sat up.

A man came forward wearing purple Hell Armor. I questioned, "Michael?"

More beings in Hell Armor surrounded me. This didn't look good. The land formed around me into a burnt-down forest filled with fog. The fog was so thick. It was getting harder to see what was in front of me.

I used Scan to to see what was going on. They all had the same aura signature as Michael. Each Demon Slayer was a different size. I believe one of them was a female. It appeared that Michael was not alone after all.

The one in the center asked, "Do you think you're worthy?"

I responded, "Worthy of what?"

The one in the center took off his helmet. He looked like James did but with white hair and was seventy years old. The man in the center spit in the Void. His eyes turned purple and put his helmet back on. I stood there naked trying to figure out what was going on. I felt so vulnerable.

The Demon Slayers charged me fast and kicked me in unison. I was surrounded by burning feet. Their speed was immense. Each slayer took turns beating the hell out of me. I had never experienced a blessing like this before.

My body was taking blow after blow until I couldn't move anymore. This was insane. How was I supposed to beat this many slayers? I counted how many there were. There were twelve altogether.

As they charged me, vines came out of the ground and grabbed them hoisting them into the air. The trees around me came to my aid. The fight was becoming fair as long as the trees restrained them. I teleported to the female Demon Slayers and punched her in the face. Each blow slowly breaking her Hell Armor helmet off. The girl looked at me. She had red hair and elven ears like my own. I would say she looks just like me. It was too early to tell if this was a dream. I just saw my own reflection in Demon Slayer form.

I repeatedly hit the Demon Slayer. The other slayers were breaking free. I had a one track mind and didn't notice. A slayers got behind me in mid-swing and held my arm back. They took their other hand and slammed into my back over and over again.

The Demon Slayer threw me on the ground and whipped out two swords. He stabbed me in the chest piecing through my breast. This was the Void so death wasn't an option. Pain, however, was forced upon me. This was not good as a golden pool of blood was coming out. I could feel my chest caving in as I couldn't breathe.

The blood was destroying the blades from the Demon Slayer. I tried to run away, but two more Demon Slayers ran at me and kicked me hard. I was flying across the forest. I needed to find sanctuary.

From above us, was a bright light that slowly came down. The source was Angela. Her wings were sprawled out and gracefully fell to the ground. The light seemed to hurt the Demon Slayers. Their armor was falling off and their skin was burning.

The eldest Demon Slayer said, "You can not interfere. This is Demon Slayer business. She has to be chosen by the clan. There is no avoiding this."

Angela replied, "So what is your verdict. She still stands, doesn't she? Twelve against one doesn't seem like good odds."

The Demon Slayer replied, "The only way to say yes is if the other is dead. The first choice must be destroyed for he is the chosen of all Demon Slayers."

Angela said, "His choices are just. Your choice is not wise nor a good fit. She forms the way you wish that she could. Things have to change to win the last battle. Don't you agree?"

My wounds healed up fast. This must be the way Michael and Paine feel. They always heal fast, but always feel the effects. Who is the girl they are talking about before me? Is this a Michael thing?

The Demon Slayer said, "This is ours to decide. God doesn't get to decide."

Angela replied, "God always chooses in the end. I'm not sure why this matters. He is going to kill you all eventually. We all know this."

I asked, "Who will kill them?"

Angela replied, "Stay out of this child. There is way too much to know and you need to go home."

The forest disappeared. The Demon Slayer had crossed arms. I fell through the air down to my body. The fall was intense. I wasn't used to falls like this. I felt sick to my stomach. My arms reach out to slow the fall. It didn't help at all. I dropped back into my body.

I hit the pavement hard and cracked it a little. What the hell just happened? Michael stood there with a smile on his face. I walked over to him. I don't know why, but lost control. My hand slapped Michael in the face as hard as I could. The slap left quite a mark on him. I stormed out of the church.

Michael looked puzzled. He said, "What did I do?"

Chapter 14

As I stormed out of the church, I felt a weird pain in my chest. Onyx followed me as I walked back to the room. I felt the heat taking over me. I needed water. The room was on the top floor which was becoming a pain in the ass.

I got up there and the room was hot. This was just great. I don't know why it was cool this whole time, but now it's warm. I ran over and laid in bed. The heat was getting to me. Onyx sat down beside me.

Onyx twisted her collar around a bit. It was rubbing a little which didn't hurt her. The collar was driving her crazy. She emitted a cool breeze from her body. The room began to feel like air conditioning. It was her the whole time. I was grateful that she was there.

I closed my eyes and enjoyed the cool breeze coming across me. She was sitting there next to me waiting to talk. I don't think we had a real conversation yet. I looked over at her. Her cheeks were getting a little blue. The slightest bit of power was causing her skin to change. Her aura was ice itself. I can see now what Paine saw. How is he so good at telling strengths?

Onyx said, "I'm here if you need to talk. The group was in shock. This moment seemed like girl talk more than anything. I have a feeling it has to do with something your angel told you."

I asked, "Girl talk?"

Onyx replied, "Girl talk."

I said, "You got wine."

Onyx responded, "I wish, but no. I'm just here as an ear. Chavez believes in you people. I am taking a leap of faith based on the awkward moment I had with Paine."

I laughed and snarkily said, "You mean when you tried to fuck Paine. We all saw. Just keep a level head."

Onyx got colder and was freezing me a bit. She gets that way when she is angry about something. Onyx was a little impulsive. That seemed to be a character trait most of us shared.

I said, "It had nothing to do with what my angel told me. It has everything to do with what she didn't tell me. I was attacked in the Void. It was by people just like Michael. I don't know why. They seemed to claim that someone had to die for me to be number one. I have no idea what it meant."

Onyx said, "You met the Demon Slayer ancestors."

I asked, "What do you mean and how did you know that?"

Onyx smiled and replied, "I know a bit from a Demon Slayer that destroyed my village. They don't fight alone. Demon Slayers run in packs. The fact that he is alone right now is crazy weird. There is a reason they are the most feared class in the world.

I can only guess that Michael has imprinted upon you people instead of his clan. There seems to be a weird thing when Demon Slayers meet each other. Chaos becomes a part of their lives. Demon Slayers become savage and primal. Their main goal is to procreate until a powerful being takes them away from the pack."

I said, "So they saw me as a powerful being. I'm not that powerful."

Onyx said, "You managed to use your force to turn the animals into Kaiju. That is only done among the most powerful Beast Tamers in the world. The only thing you lack now is defense. Lift up your shirt."

I lifted my shirt and there were two glowing marks from where they stabbed. I felt the cuts deep inside of me. The pain wasn't there, but the glow stayed. I was imprinted with something. My mind was worrying about what was happening to me. My muscles were rippling like they had a six-pack.

Onyx said, "You're an elf, one of the original races of Demon Slayers. You will certainly match him. I just hope you realize that more is going to happen. To mate with a Demon Slayer is like mating with the devil himself. You don't know if you'll get a demon or an acolyte."

I asked, "Well we aren't even close enough for that stage yet."

Onyx replied, "Sweety, he is a fifteen-year-old boy. The fact that he hasn't tried yet is astounding. Demon Slayers have a ravenous appetite for sex when drawn to a woman. They imprint on them and desire sex with that person for the rest of their lives. The downside is when they die. The Demon Slayers go on rampages. Michael will be no different."

I asked, "How do you know all this?"

Onyx said, "I fell in love with one once. He died from a group of priests trying to protect me. The priests sold me into slavery. That's how I ended up with five different masters until Paine. I met Chavez at the third master. We maimed him until he couldn't fight back anymore."

I said, "Good luck maiming Paine. The man was cut in half and still managed to survive."

Onyx said, "I know. So what is up with Darwin? The man was strange from the very beginning."

I replied, "A person can change in a sixty-year span. Especially when he is given a mirror that is indestructible."

Onyx asked, "What does that mean?"

I said, "The man was forced to look in the mirror for over sixty years. He seemed to have some sort of resentment toward black people. The guy was severely racist toward his own kind which is weird. The only way that happens is if a person was racist before he got here. Or his racist tendencies was learned behavior once he got here.

The realization that you either die or accept what you are, is a breaking point. The Void Storage is completely controlled by Paine. The guy probably tried to kill himself a few times. I don't know how long, but he went through the five stages of grief. The end result is that he learned to accept what he was.

Darwin spent sixty years in an black abyss. He was building on very little mana. When he came to terms with things, Paine let him out. The experience taught him many things. It wasn't about reading blueprints. It was about evolving as a person."

Onyx replied, "Makes me want to pity him."

I said, "Don't do that. That just leads to pity sex, and I went down that road in college."

Onyx asked, "Do you know what's next?"

I replied, "What is next I think is Megan's training. We can't leave the city and she is going to have a hard time out in the world as a level one. The way priests described her. One day, she will be able to take down Michael with ease. I just hope they are right."

The cool breeze from Onyx was great. The girl could really talk. I mean really talk. I just wanted to get some sleep. Our conversation was nice. I missed the days when Mercedi and I would drink wine and do this. Those were great nights.

I rolled over and went to sleep. Onyx went to her bed and just lay there crying. I have no idea why. She never once mentioned to me anything sad. As a woman, it is hard to understand women sometimes. All I could do was be supportive when I wasn't exhausted.

I woke up in the room due to a glowing bright light. I was having a really hard time sleeping and looked over. Megan was glowing. I'm not talking a little glow, but a big one. She was punching the air. Paine started her training up there. That's not good. With her being untapped properly, she might blow a hole in the side of the building.

I said, "What the hell are you doing?"

Paine said, "Training."

I replied, "Use your head! She hasn't learned control yet. Megan could blow the building up!"

Sometimes men don't think. Loraine looked at Paine with a told you so look. Paine put his head down and walked outside with Megan. I don't know why he thinks these things are okay. The man got into a habit of doing whatever he wanted. With his vast wealth, Paine was paying off anything that happened.

I got out of bed and went outside. The sun was bright and hard to see. I walked through town to see if the markets were going to have good food for the group.

A guard came over to me and asked for my name. I told him not seeing who he was. His visor was down and shined on me so bright. I was going blind. He asked me to follow him.

I didn't have my team. This might be worrisome. I was stuck here while the wyrms were eating corpses. I couldn't escape the city. The king was done playing nice guy now that we defeated the goblins.

I walked through the gate and up the stairs to the throne room. Augustus, David, and Solomon stood before me. To my right was Matilda. This seemed to be a council of royalty. I needed to be on my A game. Solomon seemed to be the smartest in the group.

Augustus asked, "Do you know why I have summoned you here?"

I replied, "No, but I assume it has to do with my title as Princess of Tryanon."

Augustus answered, "Yes and no. You see your sister left the city to head to the city of Braun. Normally, I wouldn't care but things have been happening there. People seem to be going missing everyday. It is believed that Beelzebub is in the Forest of the Mists as we speak."

I said, "Matilda has been there before. She had a mission to help the dwarves there a year ago. Seeing an old friend is not a crime."

Augustus replied, "But joining the Demon Lord's army is. There are rules set in place for a reason. Normally, we would just kill someone who is suspected of this, but since she is royalty. We have to make sure. The last thing we need is a war over a mistake."

I replied, "Matilda is a horrible person. I'll give you that. A person in the Demon Lord's army. Not a chance in hell. She is too much of a control freak to allow anyone to control her.

Everything she says or does is to control everyone around her. If she was on Beelzebub's side. Don't you think she would have just let the goblins run rampant in the city? She was literally the only reason that we kept them from the wall most of the fight. That's the best part of being a weather witch."

Solomon rebutted, "Goblins running the city and barely fighting would be a great way to help us drop our guard. The truth was the fight was really easy compared to what it should have been. We had a one in fifteen million chance of winning. The casualties were minimal. Only a thousand people died which is excellent for a battle of this magnitude.

The hive mind could have killed so much more. This means there was a plan in place. Our scouts are trying to figure out the next move. Her possible involvement worries us.

Matilda being a high-level person of Tryanon. That could mean disaster if Draco isn't on his toes. Matilda's involvement could also destroy your city and weaken it. Evil could spread through your city like wildfire. The devil will own your city again. The damage would be far worse this time around."

The political war was happening right now. I needed to save Matilda. She was leaning against the wall not realizing how severe this could get. It also could mean that she didn't care. Matilda thought that taking them all on was her way of having fun.

Matilda's bloodlust has been easier to spot lately. I would have never guessed that she would be involved in the affairs of a Demon Lord General. I tried to play along, but she was looking guilty at this point.

I asked, "Matilda, what were you doing in Braun?"

Matilda replied, "None of your fucking business."

Well, that response wasn't good. I'm trying to defend her life. This was turning into a mess. I closed my eyes and tried to think clearly. They were testing me to see if I had anything to do with it.

I said, "If you don't have any proof of wrongdoing. I ask that you let us leave. We are going to be stuck in this city and only two of us can fly."

Augustus said, "You really think I would get you all the way here just to discuss her possible treason. I need to know if Michael has imprinted on anyone. It seems that he hasn't met any of his kind yet which usually leads to disaster. There are talks of another female Demon Slayer in this world. If these two match up, Their power might be too much for a kingdom to handle."

I replied, "I'm not sure how a person can be imprinted upon. So I'm guessing no."

Solomon answered, "A Demon Slayer has to choose a mate. When they do, they will try to mate in a procreation fashion. That means the person has been chosen as a soul mate to them. After this, the Demon Slayer would rather die than betray them. Demon Slayers are very loyal, but if the mate is a bad person. That will lead to serious consequences."

I said, "Well unless Matilda has fucked him. He has not been imprinted yet. Unless a blow job counts."

Solomon said, "I don't believe it does. There haven't been any tests on this. I just know what the texts say about it. It just says sex. They have to be willing to create a Hellspawn."

I replied, "That's a crude way to say it."

Solomon rebutted, "That is what is told. The texts are old so there might be a bias toward things a bit. A demon-creating demon children doesn't seem too far off. The point is that when you have a demon the best course of action is balance. The preferred way would be an angel. Since nobody is an angel on earth we have the next best thing a good person with values."

I said, "The only real good woman in the group is Loraine and she is taken by Paine."

David said, "Loraine is good, but a priest would probably just gross him out. We are looking at you to mate with him. The thing is you seem to love him. Sources tell us you even stalk him a bit. So it's either you love him as a brother and watch over him like a child. Or you love him as a mate and want him for yourself. Paine and I communicate about these issues. We have been pen pals for years."

I replied, "So Paine is a mole to the kingdom."

David rebutted, "We are just two friends that talk. Paine is the reason we didn't attack your country during the king shift. I feel fortunate that we didn't as the war with goblins was coming. The thing is you need to see him as a diplomat that does what is needed to keep peace in the kingdoms. One day, you may need us to defend Tryanon."

Matilda looked at me coldly. These were discussions that she didn't want to hear. Unfortunately, she now knows how to control Michael. All she has to do is fuck Michael. He would be putty in her hands. This was going to be rough since she already had his favor.

Augustus said, "Well since I am not convinced by either of you that Matilda isn't conspiring against the kingdoms. Matilda is to be locked up in our special dungeon until we get to the bottom of this."

I said, "That doesn't seem fair to imprison a princess. Do you normally put princesses in dungeons for no reason?"

Augustus replied, "The special dungeons are for royalty being put on trial. Matilda will have the most comfortable bedroom but will get stuck in there until we see she if is fit to come out. She will have the best food in the kingdom. Matilda will most assuredly be well taken care of."

Matilda realized that she was going to be trapped. This was a fate worse than death for her. A Barbarian was going to make sure she wouldn't leave a location. Her freedom was in question and worst of all. Matilda wasn't in control.

I really hope that I'm getting better at this political stuff. Because if not, I would say Matilda's doomed. Normally, I might feel sad about it, but she's a cunt. I wanted to see her squirm.

The guards came over and escorted Matilda out of the room to her new chambers. I looked at the trinity of men as if they were coming after me next. I was still there. There was no sign of them getting ready to dismiss me.

Augustus said, "What do you two think?"

Solomon replied, "Matilda is definitely doing something behind the scenes. I'm not entirely sure of what, but she spoke to someone. If we are lucky, it wasn't Beelzebub. The last thing we need is that monster in our case.

As for Isabella, I see her as pure for the most part. Isabella is damaged in many ways. But heroes are always damaged. As for whether she would be a good imprint. I think so.

Isabella seems cunning in her own way. The fact that her heart isn't afraid of him, but drawn to him tells us about Michael himself. The fact that David took forever to see him as a Demon Slayer tells even more. Do I think he should imprint on her? The answer is yes. Keeping Matilda in the dungeons will give her more opportunities to mate with him.

Isabella was right about one thing. They are stuck here until the wyrms outside eat all the leftover dead bodies. Their friend Luas has been at the gate doing some sort of vampire thing where he eats all their blood, which is gross, but will allow the worms to not stick around as long.

Paine went down there to do the same with his Ability Syphon, but apparently, that only works on the living. I haven't learned that one yet. I found it to be fascinating. Can't wait for it.

What do you say Isabella will you mate with the Demon Slayer?"

Chapter 15

The royals let me leave the throne room. I needed to decide what to do next. I wasn't sure whether or not to take the next step. I knew that I loved him and always have, but procreation at my age was a huge step. I barely got to live, Fuck fuck fuck fuck, okay. I will just have to you know get up the nerve first.

I always wanted him to be my mate so there shouldn't be much in the way of pressure right. I mean he has his flaws. BOY does he have flaws, but I love him anyway. It's the fifteen thing. It has to be. I am so much older and wiser this time at fifteen or am I going to make the same mistake all over again.

The king actually rooted for me a bit. They seem to think I'm the best choice. How am I the best choice? He likes my sister more. The fact that they see her as a threat might be a problem. Maybe I should let her. The king sees me as less of a threat. I feel like a political pawn right now.

The king seems to believe I should give up my virginity for the sake of both kingdoms. That is a crazy thought in itself. The last time I lost my virginity it was a horrible experience that I never wanted to talk about again.

I went to the tavern to see if people were eating there. The whole crew was there. Michael was laughing and drinking a lot. He was very hammered. Michael saw me and raised his hand. I needed to not seem obvious, but I had plans for us tonight.

I sat down at the table and asked for a salad and an ale. I needed to get a little tipsy to do this. Otherwise, I might not have the courage to do it.

I liked the salads here. They are picked fresh from the northeast farms every day. I even believe there is a garden on their roof. The carrots are rare, but they always have enough for my salad.

Paine said, "I heard you went to see the king today. How did it go?"

I replied, "Well, they seem to think that Matilda is conspiring against the kingdoms. She is being put in a special dungeon until things get worked out."

Michael had an angry look on his face and exclaimed, "That is outrageous!"

Paine responded, "Relax brother. She said special dungeon. The girl will be in a bedroom being catered to until her time is up. The only difference is she can't leave. The special dungeons are a place I wouldn't mind visiting. They are just used to contain special people. Some are even put there to prevent assassination attempts."

Michael said, "So no torture."

Paine replied, "No torture, Unless you count people waiting on you hand and foot torture."

Michael looked deeply disappointed. I thought he was going to be happy she was okay. The city was making him antsy and he wanted to do fun stuff, but was stuck there since he was the only flyer in the group. Well, besides Matilda, but she would rather die than carry any of us.

I drank my ale fast and finished my salad. I choked a little bit on the salad and did my best not to look Michael in the eyes. I needed to work on this slowly. My nerves were shot and the group noticed. I wasn't being my normal snarky self. I had a look like I was about to cry.

The group got up from the table, but Michael stayed behind. I put my head down and looked at the door. They all left to go train. Michael scooted down the table in front of me. He crossed his arms and propped them on the table. Michael sat his chin down and stared at me. He knew something was up. We had been there for each other for six years. We were best friends.

Michael took his left hand and stroked my hair a bit. I don't know why, but I loved the feeling of having my hair played with and he knew it. Michael kept stroking and wrapping his fingers ever so gently around my ears. The sensation from my ears always put me in a frenzy. I would feel warm and breathe heavily. Most of the time, playing with my ears made me want to jump his bones. That was unless I was really pissed off.

Michael said, "I'm not sure what happened, but I'm here for you. Sounds like Matilda will be fine."

I replied, "It's not that at all. A part of me is glad she is out of our lives for a little while."

Michael asked, "So what is the problem?"

I exclaimed, "You are the problem!"

Michael was very confused and raised his voice a little saying, "Me! What did I do!?"

Michael raised his head off the table. His eyebrows were raised and his eyes looked like they were about to bulge out of his head. He looked concerned but didn't realize it wasn't his fault.

Michael was looking to see what the problem was. This sucks because he deserves better than me. Especially when the reason comes out why I'm doing this so soon. Maybe he will be okay with it.

I said, "It's not really your fault. I just have to deal with things on my own."

Michael replied, "You never have to deal with things alone when I'm around. If you need help with anything just talk to me. I'll try to be a good listener."

Michael saw the tavern people bring in a bunch of meat from the slaughter of a cow. His mouth was salivating as he thought about his meal tonight. He did his best at least. The boy just seems to think about food at these times. It was going to take them a few hours to prepare and he chose to focus on the steak instead.

I said, "We can get that tonight."

Michael said, "Yeah. Paine needs to know about this. It looks delicious. He might buy the whole cow."

I replied, "I mean just you and me. Alone eating here."

Michael looked puzzled. The idea of us eating together without the group didn't cross his mind at all. He was thinking about how Paine would save all the meat for later. I was thinking about how I was going to get him to form a bond with me. Why are men simple and difficult all at the same time?

Michael got up from the table and said, "I'm going to see if Paine has some apples for me. It's a date tonight. I'll be here ready to eat. You better be ready to eat steak too. No more vegetables. You'll turn into a carrot at this point."

Michael left the tavern. Turn into a carrot. What the hell did that mean? Whatever, it took me way too long to realize. He accepted my invitation for a date tonight. I was excited and wanted to leap inside. My time was coming, but did he know he accepted a date. I guess I'll find out tonight.

I left the tavern and walked down the street a bit. There was Paine and Loraine picking out food for the group. Paine would store all of food in his storage. He had enough gold to feed the group for a hundred lifetimes. He didn't care about the gold as he was actually low maintenance except for his clothing cost. That man had to own a million shirts from Wong.

I said, "Loraine" and waved at her. She saw me and smiled. Loraine waved me over and pointed to some apples at the stand. Did Michael really eat all the apples? Paine had so many of them that I thought they would never run out.

Paine said, "I will take your apples."

The merchant asked him how many. Paine had a weird saying. Whenever he wanted something for the storage. He would just buy all of it.

Paine said, "I want all your apples. Now I know you think that I said I want a lot of apples, but what I'm asking for is ALL your apples."

The merchants would overcharge for the apples, but Paine saw it as a good product. He also didn't have to waste time finding other vendors. The man valued his time. Especially since he was training over half the group.

I said, "When you're done with him can we talk."

Loraine looked puzzled and asked, "What did Paine do this time?"

I replied, "He did nothing. I just want to...Girl talk."

Loraine face changed. Her eyes got wider. She acted like what I said was shocking beyond belief.

Loraine said, "Baby you got this. I'm in need. Don't forget to pick up Megan later. Onyx and Chavez are not her masters."

Paine yelled, "I know dear." As we walked away.

Loraine said, "So what is going on. Something seemed really off at the tavern. Michael said.

Does that mean you guys are going on a date finally? I wasn't sure it would ever happen since you're brooding all the time."

I exclaimed, "I'm not brooding. I'm just growing up and acting less juvenile. A lot is going on and I just wish to be on top of things."

Loraine said, " Are we waiting for privacy? I want the juicy details."

I stayed somewhat silent, but Loraine was jovial about the whole thing. I never really thought of myself as brooding, but maybe she is right. I'm like a mother trying to round up all her children.

Loraine and I got into the inn. I went upstairs and got into the room. The maid was doing the sheets and blankets. The place was great for what we needed, but what I really needed was a quiet time with her. The maid left the room immediately. She didn't want to interfere with our talking I'm guessing.

I sat down on my bed and Loraine sat across from me. She smiled and said, "Now, nobody is here. Spill the damn beans already."

I said, "I'm thinking of asking if Michael wants to be my mate. Do you know anything about this process?"

Loraine's arms tucked in and shook in excitement. This was a big day in her eyes. That means she would be a part of our joint union. Since there weren't many of us in the group. The joining of two group members is serious.

Loraine said, "So you know the mating thing with Demon Slayers right. There is no going back. He will follow you like a lost puppy for the rest of his life. They only find one mate in their whole lives. So if this is some childish game.....Don't! You will destroy him forever and it could unleash something awful."

I replied, "It's real. Has been for a long time. I mean he irritates me, but I love Michael. He does stupid stuff but doesn't mean to hurt anyone. Michael has been a huge part of my life. He is the only person that has stood by me in my life. Yeah, he is kind of dumb, but there is a weird charm about it. He is also controlling himself better."

Loraine laughed and said, "You just described all men. If you are getting ready to mate though. These guys are hard to deal with. I have been trying for years with Paine. He doesn't budge. If you get the chance too, you might have just improved the chances for the rest of the group."

I asked, "So...how would you do this?"

Loraine replied, "Well get him the best food imaginable. He will gladly tell you since the boy can't keep his mouth shut. I would make sure there is enough liquor that he can't say no easily. The night will move on and before you know it. You're doing the horizontal mambo. I would rent a private room too. The last thing you need is one of us ruining your big night."

I said, "The private room would have to be the best advice you ever gave in your life."

We both laughed at it, but it really was. Paine didn't know what the word privacy meant. He didn't do it on purpose but walked over while Loraine was bathing one time and asked her if she wanted anything picked up. The guy didn't take a hint and just stared at her naked. At first, I thought he was just a perv, but Loraine assured me she had offered him more than just a peek for years.

The day was ending and I walked down to the tavern. The meat was ready to be served. Paine came in there and bought all of it, but was kind enough to buy our diner. He made sure the group had some liquor. He bought a whole keg to bring to the room. People walked in and were pissed not realizing that the meat was already sold out.

I put on my white dress. I still fit in the thing all these years. The larger size back then was a good choice. I sat at a table and waited for him. Paine was at the door talking to him. Michael came into the room in a tuxedo. I can't believe Paine made him wear a tuxedo. That means he might know something after all.

Michael sat down at the table with me. He looked really nervous and uncomfortable. He looked around at the stuff he saw a million times before. We went into the tavern every day to eat. What the hell was he looking for?

Michael said, "This is weird, right. I have never worn a tuxedo in my whole life. Paine insisted that I wear one. Loraine was laughing the whole time. I just wanted to eat some good meat. Anyway, they said you wanted to talk about something."

I froze for a bit. The pressure was really getting to me. My face was turning red in embarrassment. My heart was racing a mile a minute. I could feel my eyes watering. I couldn't help but wonder if this was going to be a bad omen.

I said, "I came to talk to you tonight about something weird."

Michael replied, "I'm all for weird. I haven't had any excitement around here in a long time. Until the wyrms and Lucas are done cleaning up nobody is allowed in or out of the kingdom. What did you have in mind?"

I swallowed a lot of spit. This was so much harder than I thought. He seems to be sincere and I can't get the words to come out. I ended up spouting out the first thing that came to mind.

I asked, "Do you remember what you said to me when you jumped off that wall?"

Michael couldn't remember. He was trying to think until eventually he got it. He replied, "You talking about when you got wrapped up in the moment and told me you loved me. That took me off guard, but I realized you didn't mean it. You just said that because it could have been the last time you saw me. So I had to think of the best response possible. I can't remember what it was, but I remember laughing about it as I jumped off the wall."

I said, "It was I know. You said I know. Do you know how humiliating that was? I confessed love to you and you shrugged it off like it was nothing."

At that moment, Michael realized he messed up. He just stared at the table. He didn't think the confession was real.

The food came out. He started to eat the steak. He was enjoying it but got a spot of blood on his suit. I took my thumb and licked it trying to get the stain off. Michael swallowed hard and realized something. He never told me what it was but his face softened and gazed deep into my eye. His purple eyes were mesmerizing. I couldn't say a word.

Michael asked, "What is it that you wanted to talk to me about? Are we here to give each other a real confession of love? I don't know if I'm ready for love."

I said, "I'm not here to ask about love. We both know that our feelings or at least mine far surpass that. I'm asking for you to mate with me."

Michael just about fell out of his chair. His eyes grew big. I could hear his heart going wild. This was definitely not what he was expecting. He kept feeling the area on his face where the horns were coming out. I think the sensation that brings them out are similar stressors.

I said, "I rented a room already. I'm just waiting for your answer."

Michael looked at his food and lost his appetite. I wasn't sure if this was a good sign or not. I couldn't figure out if it was butterflies in his stomach or whether the idea repulsed him. Michael didn't realize how severe this really was. He didn't know much about his kind. I kind of felt bad about rushing him into it.

Michael said, "If we do this. Nothing changes. We fight and defeat the Demon Lord. If we have a child, our goal will be to get stronger to defend the child from the Demon Lord. If you promise this, I will be okay with it. All I know right now is that I made a promise to my father to defeat the Demon Lord. It's what God will."

I nodded my head yes. This was being expedited for political reasons. I was really nervous myself. I knew that I loved him. I knew that nothing would stop me from loving him. Michael was a wild animal that needed help to be tamed.

We left the tavern and went to our private room. I remember this night so well. Michael was trying to take off the tuxedo. His hands were so large that he couldn't properly get the buttons to unbutton. I laughed at it, but it was so endearing.

Michael's clothes were completely off. Now it was my turn. I was shaking badly, but I really wanted this to happen. He stripped off the straps from my dress allowing my breasts to be exposed. They grew quite a bit from when I was nine.

I stood there before him naked stiff as a board. He wasn't sure what to do at all. It had been so long since any of us did anything that we were kind of lost. I grabbed his hand and sat him on the bed. His legs were shaking so bad that the bed sounded like we were already having sex.

I sat on Michael's lap. His legs were still moving so there was still a bit of stimulation. Michael grabbed me from behind my ears and pulled me for the most passionate kiss I ever got. I was stunned and didn't wish to be let go. Michael kept rubbing them stimulating my senses.

I wrapped my legs around his waist to pull him in tighter. My arms were wrapped around under his arms. I kissed for so long that I could hardly breathe. My mind didn't care that it was feeling lightheaded. I wanted more.

Michael pulled away and was in shock. He wasn't just a little erect. Michael got so big that I think he felt a little pain. I could see it in his face. His eyes lit up as if it was Christmas morning. He smiled like he was about to open all of his presents. It was one hell of a present to open if I do say so myself.

I violently pushed him back on the bed. Michael was enjoying my forceful nature. His legs were dangling off the bed and flew us both up slightly and properly placed us on the bed. This was the moment of truth.

I got myself above him trying to properly line up his penis to me. Michael was so big that it was just gliding against the outside. Not exactly the way I thought this was going to go, but it was a work in progress.

I dropped down and tried to push it in. I felt a sharp piercing feeling. The shock went up my spine and shook me to my very core. Michael was barely in. I was just worried that he was going to take control.

My legs were in a squatting position. I went up and down a few times. The tip was goin in. I was feeling the sharp pain still. Over time the pain subsided. I was in pure ecstasy. The weird mix of pain and pleasure was driving me wild.

My eyes rolled into the back of my head. I kept moaning every time I dropped down. I saw some blood coming from me, but I don't think he noticed at all.

Michael was trying to be gentle with me and held my waist. He went up and didn't allow me to just graze the tip anymore. I couldn't believe that after all these years. I was actually having sex with him. I tried to replicate the move I had in my first life. My hips were going back and forth riding him like a cowgirl.

Michael stopped holding onto my waist and let me take control. His arms were at his side. Michael was pulling his hands back to grab the headboard. His muscles were bulging and making him look more massive. I was having the best moment of my life.

My movement eventually worked my way down to take on the whole thing. I was in a lot of pain, but also in a lot of pleasure. I never wanted this moment to end. I was taking charge of the whole thing. Michael was loving it but wasn't going to let things happen this way.

Michael sat up and grabbed me by the waist flipping me over. I was on the bottom now. My arms were up in the air pushing him away. He grabbed my hands and pushed them. Michael went in deep making me feel a sensation that was never there before. He leaned down and grabbed my ears rubbing them once again. Michael dove in for another passionate kiss. The muscles on his chest were tensing up. I never thought I could feel this much... man before in my life. Only word I could think of.

Michael pulled back and grabbed the headboard. He started off slow but got stronger. Each trust was so strong that I was getting pushed into the headboard. Every inch of his throbbing cock was going inside. Sweat drenched the bed as passion enthralled us both. I moaned with each thrust. I couldn't help it.

We had to stop and adjust ourselves since he kept thrusting my head into the headboard. Luckily it was there, because at the rate we were going. Michael might have fucked me into the next room. He gained his rhythm as the screeching and pounding on the headboard helped him.

I believed at that moment Michael loved me from the moment we met. He just never showed his affections properly. Michael's body tensed up. His eyes lit up. Michael bit into my neck drawing blood. I realized I might be kinky because I really enjoy that. The pain mixed with the pleasure was building my adrenaline rush.

I pulled Michael in closer and wrapped my legs around him. He just kept moving the best way he could. My hands grabbed onto his back and pulled him in. I was scrapping his back causing his purple blood to drip out slowly.

Michael didn't seem to mind in fact he was getting off on it as I kept scratching him with my nails. He kept healing immediately. Michael's adrenaline was so bad that he treated sex like it was war. I was loving it. The blood was dripping onto the bed. Michael sat up and saw what happened.

Michael said, "I hope we don't have to pay for those sheets."

I replied, "Just get down here you idiot."

I yanked him down and gave him a passionate kiss. This was me fighting back. Sex in our relationship was always a battle of will. Sometimes he won, most of the time I won. We loved every minute of it.

I could feel Michael's penis getting ready to go off. I let him go for a moment. He fucked me as hard as he could. My vagina was black and blue. I had a hard time walking for quite some time. Michael thrust into me and came for the first time. We went at it like animals for over thirty minutes. I was never going to let this one go.

Michael rolled off of me and sprawled across the bed. He just stared at the ceiling trying to get his bearings back. He looked over at me sweating so bad that I could smell him. Strangely enough. Michael often smelled like cotton candy.

Michael before he shut his eyes said, "I love you, too."

Chapter 16

A month had passed and Lucas was done cleaning up the dead bodies. The wyrms kept searching for more bodies but realized that there was no more and ran away. When the bodies were gone the guards were attacking the wyrms to scare them away.

The best part of being in Zahn. I didn't have to do anything. It was like a relaxing vacation. I really needed to learn to let loose. My whole life my father tried to get me to loosen up. I refused out of spite.

I was called to the king for formal greetings. He never once offered us a room. It really would have cheapened my room fees as we kept the room for the rest of the month. We had to buy six replacement beds in that time period. Yeah, you heard me six.

Michael didn't like the number six so he bought two more and had Paine store them. I asked why we didn't just have sex in there. Michael told me that Paine sees and hears everything going on in that Void Storage.

A part of me is glad he knew that and was thinking about our privacy. After a month of doing everything under the sun. I wouldn't mind being watched a little bit. It might have added some spice.

Megan trained in the Void Storage for a total of six hundred years. If you didn't figure things out. That makes Megan older than both of us in a weird way. Her level was getting up there. Since she had no kills at all. I believe she only hit a hundred-something.

Megan ended up getting like twenty-something skills, but we aren't allowed to know about them yet. Paine is keeping everyone's new skills a secret. I wasn't sure as to why he chose this path. He didn't seem to trust someone. Matilda was locked up so it couldn't have been her.

Diego and Sylvia were staying in our room, because they go with me everywhere. I keep forgetting how young they actually are. Diego walked over to me the other day. He had this sad look on his face.

Diego said, "If I am forced to see you two fucking one more time. I'm cutting out my own eyes. I understand you two are in love, but as your guardians, we have to watch you closely. It is grossing us out."

Sylvia heard him say that and bit his neck. She scolded him and said how beautiful everything was. The lovemaking, biting, scratching, and noises were all part of the primal experience. They do the same thing except for the lovemaking. I'm glad that is addressed since they are brother and sister. That would be weird.

I was so glad the month was up. Sort of. Michael won't get to play around as much, but we can finally do quests again. We walked as a group down to the local guild. There seemed to be no quests that we could take without joining their guilds. I figured we would just go in there and test with flying colors for a new quest.

Paine was being just that. A pain in the butt because he refused. It was like he was looking for a particular quest. After visiting five guilds, he stood in the middle of town. He shot a Void Sphere into the air and watched it blow up.

A group of guards came ran to him and drew their swords. It looked like he was trying to attack the kingdom and it worked. Unfortunately, he might be getting us all thrown into jail. I raised up my hands. The guards kept screaming.

Paine said, "Take me to David. I have things to discuss."

One of the guards recognized him as the paladin that saved the city. He told all of them to drop their swords. When you see Paine ruthlessly stab himself to death and make an atomic bomb with your blood. You try to come up with a resolution quickly.

The guards took us into the castle and toward a courtyard. David was in there staring at the sun. What a weird thing for a blind man to do! He sat in a chair with a tea kettle and cups. There seemed to be enough cups for everyone in the group.

David said, "You can sure make an entrance. I always dig that about you. You scared the shit out of my guards."

Paine replied, "I never stray away from a fight. I'm here because of that discussion we had. The quest that matches Matilda's release."

David said, "Oh right, I forgot to post it. Solomon was talking about trains again and before I knew it my mind went to mush and here we are."

I asked, "There are trains in this world?"

David said, "No the last world. We all remember this stuff try to keep up."

I was a little insulted, because of course I remember them. The Creationists could have built something for the greater good. The trains were a basic use for travel in the eighteen hundreds.

"So what is the assignment?" Paine asked.

David said, "To the point, I like that. There are strange events outside Braun. The city in the mountains. Your assignment is to check it out since nobody appears to be coming back from the location. Whatever you do, Do Not enter the Forest of the Mist. Getting too close could awaken the Ents, dead, and demons."

Michael replied, "This is a lot more than I realized. We might be strong, but demons are a whole different game. I'm not sure we should take this one."

David rebutted, "If you don't, someone weaker will and I said DO NOT go in where the demons are. The dwarves put in the request because travelers have been having a hard time. If you wish to bail on them that is fine. They need to be notified. However, Matilda needs to go on this quest."

I said, "I don't mind leaving her behind. She can manage herself."

Paine said, "We will do it. If we return to Tryanon without her. It will be a World War. I would rather just do the mission and get it over with. What are the parameters? How will they know if the mission is complete?"

With those words, we accepted a mission we would regret soon enough. The group got to the gate and Lucas was standing there waiting for us. With him being a Blood Mage, and killing the way he does. The city kept a close eye on him. They were afraid he would draw the blood out of innocents because of his blood lust.

The guards dropped the bridge and let us out. Matilda was being dragged to the gate with ropes around her wrists and a gag in her mouth. I had a big smile on my face. There had to be a story behind this.

Paine asked, "What is the meaning of this? She was supposed to be well taken care of."

The guard replied, "The woman is an animal. She clawed a few servants and blinded one. Her teeth were used to bite the nose off a guard. The girl is crazy."

Michael laughed and said, "She's a cannibal. I wish there were photos for the Christmas album."

Matilda got the gag off and replied, "Fuck you, Michael"

The gate closed and we were stuck outside the walls. I hoped someone knew what direction we were to go in. The sand was blowing and blinding me. We all stood here for a second. Paine sat down in the sand. I think he was waiting for something.

Darwin opened a portal, popped out, and said, "I finished the little one. Just give me a second."

Darwin went back in. I heard the strangest noises. I hadn't heard these noises since the last world. I looked into the portal. A Humvee-looking vehicle came out. It was long and looked like it could carry fifteen people. There were hatches on the roof, a door in the rear, and two large doors that came out the sides.

When we opened the doors on the sides, there appeared to be a minigun on both sides. The hatches had seats to shoot from the roof and mini guns up by the engine. The rear door had another seat with a grenade launcher attached to it. The guy might have gone overboard with this.

All of us found a seat. Darwin was driving since he had to for the fuel. Paine was in the passenger seat because he called shotgun. The rest of us were in the back. The seats were so soft. I was like sitting on silk. I wanted to just sit back and fall asleep in them. Onyx and Chavez took the center seats so that if something happened they would get launched into the hatches and fire away. Michael was in the back seat with the grenade launcher. Matilda was in the driver's side door and Loraine was on the passenger side door so she could be right behind Paine.

Megan and I were in our own seats lying down like it was a comfy bed. She was giggling as we started to drive off. Hundreds of years in the Void Storage and she is still just a goofy kid.

The vehicle needed better shocks for the desert. I was bumping around and feeling sick. It wasn't being flown around at high speeds with Michael sick, but the sickness was there. In fact, I hadn't felt good for the last two weeks. Zahn was a terrible place because of their food poisoning.

The vehicle was going only forty miles an hour, but it didn't matter to me since the air conditioning was on. That is right. The boy put in air conditioning.

He was now my new favorite person. The heat in this desert was killing me since day one.

Paine yelled back, "Looks like we got a problem. There appears to be three wyrms. And we are three miles away from the land."

Onyx and Chavez went through the hatch. They were both doing nothing. I had no idea what they were waiting for. Turns out they waiting for the wyrms to get closer. Pain was the only thing that was going to slow them down. The guns needed to be close to shred.

Michael opened the back door and had a big grin on his face. He was like a kid in a candy store. Michael had his finger on the trigger but didn't pull. He was waiting for Onyx to start shooting first.

The wyrms were getting closer and the vibrations were shaking the vehicle. There wasn't a sandstorm to save us this time. Megan appeared to be scarred. I jumped over to her seat and held her closely holding her ears shut.

Onyx began to fire the minigun followed by Chavez. Chavez shot at the one on the right. Each round was covered in flames as it shot the wyrm. The fire penetrated the skin of the wyrm setting its insides on fire. You could see the smoke coming out of its mouth as it panicked to get out of the flames.

The wyrm slowed down and Chavez yelled, "That is one flame-broiled grub."

Onyx was doing the same thing with each round, but the ice was slowing down the bullets. The wyrm was slowing down as ice was attaching. The wyrm wasn't stopped and continued to charge at us.

Michael just kept repeating, "Come on baby get closer to me. Come on. Come on."

The wyrm was within twenty feet of us and Michael fired his first shot. Explosions were blowing up in the inside of its mouth. Teeth were shattering as it whimpered in pain, but it only slowed down a bit. Matilda and Loraine opened the door they were sitting in. Both of them were firing away at the center wyrm.

The skin was tough so Matilda turned her rounds into arcane rounds. Loraine couldn't transfer it into anything. The frozen wyrm was getting used to the ice. The wyrm was shattering the ice around it. Once most of it was broken, the wyrm charged at us faster than before. The wyrms were creating their own personal dust storm.

The grenade launcher and guns should have run out of round, but they didn't. Darwin's eyes were white as snow. He was using his power to generate rounds, fuel, and maintenance on the vehicle as I saw the same piece fly off three times.

The rounds were flying through the air as the middle wyrm went underground. I could feel my stomach tightening up. The wyrm with the ice on it stopped and just stood there running away. We could see the entrance to Napalm Forest.

Darwin slowed down a bit as the wyrms looked like they disappeared. Everyone closed their doors since the battle looked like it was over. People were high-fiving one another. It was a big celebration with hooting and hollering.

The wyrm in the center caught us off guard. It went underneath the vehicle and started to chew. Darwin was hitting the gas as hard as he could, but the power of the wyrm was too much. The teeth were scraping against the side of the vehicle.

Darwin kept crying out, "NO NO NO NO MY BABY!"

Darwin spent a lot of time in his garage trying to build awesome first-world projects. The man was a gem in the group, but lacking in combat. Darwin found some motivation. I think making cool stuff for the group was Darwin's way of trying to impress Onyx. He kept calling her the Ice Queen as he showed off. Wasn't much of a nickname as most people called her that.

Paine asked, "Anyone here got any good ideas."

Michael said, "Well maybe Isabella can make the hyenas in her pocket Kaiju up like at the wall. That was amazing baby."

I replied, "I can't do it right now."

Loraine said, "She can't do that for almost a year now. It takes a lot out of here to do that."

Michael replied, "Well, I can try to cut my way out. I'm not sure if my sword can break through the skin. That thing has to be ten feet thick.

There are also the mages that can destroy the inside of the wyrm. I'm not sure if we are deep underground and it could backfire. We could all become crispy critters if we can't escape."

Paine moved his hand and a large Void Storage portal opened up and we slowly went into it. The stomach stopped eating us, but we were still moving inside the belly of the beast. I got out of the vehicle and set foot in the storage.

I said, "Paine how much power will it take to keep the Void Storage open while I shoot fire arrows into its stomach."

Darwin took the vehicle into his shop and tried to think of a way to make it tunnel through the sands. Paine closed the portal. He didn't want us to see what was going on. I don't think he wanted the wyrm to take us any farther away from our final destination.

Paine said, "Let's rest for a moment, because when we are done here. Our powers need to be full-blazing. This wyrm might have swallowed us, but it will never eat us."

Paine portaled food to us. We sat down for a quick meal. Michael had fifteen apples in front of him. Paine was eating three steaks at the same time. He was starting to get a dad bod. I think Megan was part of the problem. HAHAHAHAHAHAHA!

Matilda refused to eat. She was being stubborn and had lightning creating static above her head. The electricity was flowing throughout her. Matilda was slowly losing control. I could sense a bloodlust coming from her. It was almost like she was being a demon herself.

Matilda slowly walked off into the Void Storage. Loraine was about to stop her, but Paine grabbed her arm. Paine knew something was up and wanted to protect her from something. Loraine was a little more naïve than that. She truly tried to see the good in people.

I was eating a lot. I had two steaks, three bananas, and three apples. I was really hungry all the time. I wondered at the time if it had to do with me leveling up. Loraine came over and sat beside me. She had a big grin on her face.

Loraine asked, "How are you feeling? You seem hungrier than usual. I have a sneaky suspicion I know why."

I said, "I'm just hungry. We were blessed right before we left so maybe a skill I have requires eating a lot."

Paine said, "Loraine leave her alone. If she doesn't want to talk about things. She doesn't have to. We are a family and sometimes as a family. We have to back off and let them come to us."

Those two knew something that I didn't. Maybe I had a tapeworm or something. I don't know, but Loraine couldn't stop smiling. Paine just kept eating steak. Darwin was eating the steak too.

Darwin said, "I might have modified the Sinister vehicle. It might dig us out once we get out of the wyrm's belly, but that is the problem. We need to get out of the wyrm's belly."

Michael said, "Well Paine, you want to Void Sphere us out of the side."

Paine replied, "I can rip a hole through it. The sand might come in the side, but if we don't kill it the wyrm will just eat us again."

Darwin kept staring at Onyx. He couldn't keep his eyes off her the whole time. Onyx was disgusted by it, but kind of enjoyed it at the same time. She liked the attention but hated where the attention was coming from. Onyx was disgusted by him after finding out about his past life. I should have just kept my mouth shut.

Megan was taking a nap on the ground. The Void Storage ground was soft and firm at the same time. Our bodies were warm and cozy. A nap sounded like a great idea. This place was really getting to me.

Chavez looked over at Darwin and asked, "Are you able to make food, and is it delicious? I want a quesadilla. I want to taste home again."

Darwin said, "If we find a blueprint with a quesadilla, then yes. I will make you one. Food is complicated so you would have to get every piece right and that doesn't include the meat. I can't make things out of carcasses."

I never thought Chavez would have such a sad look on his face. He really wanted his mama's cooking. Chavez had his memories of home that always put a sparkle in his eye. We all knew very little about Chavez. The only thing we knew was he loved his mom. She had the voice of an angel and could rock out to heavy metal. His words, not mine.

I could see lightning out in the distance. I think my sister was freaking out in a rage. She hated being caged. One day, I'm going to have to ask her about that. Why does she have to be in control all the time? What is with all the hate? I never sat down and thought about her as a human before. I could call it sibling rivalry, but this goes too far.

The sky kept lighting up and the stars were shifting out of the way. The stars acted like they had a mind of their own. Was this Paine's doing or was the Void sentient? The darkness was creeping in on us. If Matilda isn't careful, she will get lost.

Paine said, "We ready to do this family. We have a mission and saving queen lightning over there was the only reason we did it to begin with."

Matilda slowly walked back to the group. Her eyes were filled with hate and the next person that spoke to her was about to get struck. I chose not to say anything to her. This was not the time and for some odd reason. I started to feel defensive which isn't good if you are a hero.

Matilda came toward us striking the ground with everything she had. The streaks were lighting up the floor. It was as if the lightning was reflecting off of it. I could smell something off about her. No that wasn't a my sister stinks thing. I smelled something sickly sweet off of her. It wasn't cotton candy like Michael. It was like maybe teriyaki sauce. No, well she smelled weird. That's all I can really say about it.

Matilda walked over to us and said, "We're all going to hell. You know that right."

Chapter 17

Darwin came out of his portal. There were treads on a vehicle that looked like a cylinder. It wasn't the same vehicle as before. The front of it had a large drill bit. It was about ten feet across and designed to crush anything in its way. The bottom treads shined like silver. There was only one way in or out and that was a side panel. The inside would fit fifteen people. I wondered why he was making it so big.

Darwin hit a latch and opened the door. Smoke was coming off the machine. The inside had red silk seats with seatbelts. The seat belts didn't go across our laps but over our heads. It dropped down into a clasp.

Paine yelled, "Shotgun."

Nobody wanted the front since this vehicle was experimental and they would be the first to die if something went wrong. Paine jumped inside and the vehicle looked like it was about to fall apart. How much does that man actually weigh?

Megan went in and sat down on the way back. Her legs were kicking like mine used to. I really thought she would be more mature since she spent all that time in the Void Storage, but she didn't. Her mental status weirdly stayed the same. The Void Storage doesn't seem to improve your mental growth at all. I found that to be weird. Maybe it was because all she did was sleep, eat, and train. Everything about Paine's powers seems to be shrouded in mystery.

The rest of the group got into the drilling vehicle except me. I had to be the last to get in since I was going to strike this wyrm with fire. I pulled back my bow. Diego and Sylvia grew to normal size and shared with me their magic power. All three of us were generating a huge Fire Arrow. The spirals were generating heat. I was sweating really bad as the pressure was intensifying.

The Fire Arrow was getting larger by the second. I had to take my shot. I let go of the string on my bow. The Fire Arrow was slow. The heat was so bad that from fifteen feet away. The sides of the vehicle were bright red like it was about to melt. I could hear bells going off inside the machine.

The Fire Arrow hit the portal and was causing weird-looking disruptions. There were weird ripples in the portal that made it hard to see the other side. This wasn't good. If he doesn't keep the portal open then it could blow the inside of the Void Storage killing us all. I just watched patiently as the arrow drifted into the belly of the wyrm.

I was holding my breath in anticipation. Half the Fire Arrow worked its way through the portal. The portal was shutting down on us. All but the rear of the arrow was through. Even if it blew up, we had a chance of survival. I had a weird feeling in my stomach to run away, but I had to watch.

The Fire Arrow finally went through. The portal remained open. The second arrow sat on the side of the wyrm. Paine closed the portal. It was a jerk reaction, but a good one. Fire came through the portal like a flamethrower and was only controlled by him closing the portal up.

The vehicle door opened. Onyx and Matilda were the first to come out. They seemed to both be getting ready to cast ice spells. Onyx had an ice shield around her body, but Matilda didn't have that luxury. I stepped back and held my stomach. I must have used too much energy. I was feeling really sick.

Loraine rushed out and dropped a Mana Well and healed me. It didn't stop me from vomiting. I felt so bad. I was making a mess in Paine's Void Storage. The look on Paine's face was that of a disappointed father. It must have been that he thought I had more control.

Paine used a portal and cleaned up the messes around the Void Storage. He must have gotten used to it. The vomit disappeared and was never seen again. I did notice a weakness of his. Blood doesn't bother him in the least. When a person vomits, he looks green in the face and is about to vomit himself. You would think his healing would help him with that, but it just makes him more sick.

Onyx started to form her first Ice Wall. The reason I said, first is because there were quite a few they made together. The two of them took turns but were getting worn out from all the protection and mana they were using. The ice from the first was beginning to melt so they had to act fast and hard.

Matilda and Onyx stayed out of the vehicle as the rest of us stayed inside. I have to give Darwin credit. The vehicle seems to hold up against really high temps. The inside wasn't even affected, but the outside was slightly melted which didn't matter.

Darwin drove the drill vehicle behind the ice. Matilda and Onyx stood beside the vehicle ready for the backdraft. The oxygen in the Void is insane and would bust through destroying everything in its path. I might have used a little too much power. Now that I think about it.

Paine opened the portal. The fire melted the first wall with ease. There was a total of nine walls left. The water was spraying against it evaporating quickly. The second wall melted but stood for a few seconds the third, fourth, and fifth walls were melting at the same time.

Onyx increased her ice shield and charged her hands for burst energy. Matilda had a different approach as she is the weather witch. Matilda caused a thunderstorm to rain on the fire. The rain was helping keep the ice up longer and simmered the fire a bit. The ice was still melting. The fire was still roaring through the place. The last wall was there and Onyx was ready. The fire was burrowing through the wall. I saw the steam rolling off of the other side.

Onyx blasted it with the most chilling thing I ever saw. The ground was turning to ice. The rain Matilda was dropping was so cold it kept turning to snowflakes and dropping like water at the end. The fight with those two went on for over a minute before the fire stopped coming through the door.

The portal was finally showing the other side. The inside of the wyrm's stomach was completely set on fire. The wyrm was dying from the inside and couldn't do anything about it. We just took a moment to watch the flames burn. The vehicle wasn't going to last long if we left the Void Storage.

Michael had to wait a while with the portal open so that time would pass faster. I felt bad for the poor guy as he was using up mana for this. He had to create a large Void Sphere after to get us through the wyrm's skin since the vehicle couldn't burrow through that. Some of the flames turned blue and smoked up the wyrm's insides. We needed to find another way to get out.

As we looked, the mouth of the wyrm was opening. I was in shock to see that it went to the surface. All we had to do was get to the end out of the wyrm's mouth. Michael noticed it too. He had a huge smile on his face. His eyes turned purple a hopped out of the vehicle.

Matilda and Onyx jumped inside. Michael asked, "How resistant is this thing to heat?"

Darwin said, "There is a great deal of resistance, but we have to depend on the treads to get us through."

Michael said, "I'm more worried about Isabella's safety. The treads aren't needed."

Darwin responded, "If we could get pushed then yes. This vehicle has a lot of weight to it. A barbarian might struggle with it."

Michael stepped outside and began to push the vehicle. He lifted the back end of the vehicle up and crawled underneath. His back was holding the weight of the vehicle and all of us. Michael was carrying over ten thousand pounds worth of load. It was one of the most amazing things I ever saw him do. That boy is definitely getting lucky tonight.

Purple lightning was coming off of Michael's body. It was acting like a buffer to help him carry. Michael raised himself off the ground and began to fly. Paine opened the portal even further to help him get out more easily. I was ready for Overdrive to kick in, but he took us slowly.

Michael would have had a much easier time if he used Overdrive. I wondered why he didn't. He was thinking considerately of everyone. It always made us sick. I would vomit for a long time afterward. Maybe he knew we all had food poisoning from Zahn and didn't wish to poke the bear.

Michael flew through the center of the wyrm. The sides were blowing small fire explosions everywhere. Michael chose to not wear his armor. The heat had to be excruciating on him, but he was doing it the hard way.

The smoke was working its way out the mouth. Michael was almost to the mouth. The teeth were trying to move to pull us back into the stomach of the wyrm. Michael was dodging all of the teeth. Finally, we made it out of the wyrm's mouth. He set down the drill vehicle.

The group sat in our seats for a moment. Michael was down outside and put on his Hell Armor. He must have needed the mana. The wyrm was bellowing from all the fire and couldn't track us. It was going to die a painful death from the inside.

We backtracked less than a mile from the forest. I was glad to see that we would actually make it. Michael took off his armor. He opened the vehicle hatch coming inside. He closed the hatch and sat in front of me.

Michael plopped right there on the floor and put his head on my lap. He held me closely and looked like he was about to fall asleep in that position. I could hear him snoring a bit with a smile on his face. I remember the days were I used to do this with Michael. He would just act appalled by it.

Darwin began to use the vehicle to drive to the forest. The drill was a lot slower than the Humvee. This felt like we were only going ten miles an hour. The armor on it was a lot better so I'm thinking that until we get to the forest. This would be the best one.

The air conditioning was on, but I was crazy hot still. Everyone looked cool and relaxed. It was pissing me off. I'm going to have to stop using Elemental Arrows until I can figure out what is going on. It was like heat was trapped inside my body from it.

The group finally made it to the Napalm Forest. The entrance was quite cold. It was a quick change from land to land. The reason the place was called Napalm Forest was the trees had no problem living, but the leaves never wanted to grow. Everything in there looked like it was there was a napalm explosion that wiped everything out.

Everyone, but Darwin got out of the vehicle. He drove the drill into the garage and left it there coming out. His hand clapped and dust flew everywhere. Times like that made me ask what was going on in there.

Megan looked like she was about to cry. Her legs were a lot smaller than the rest of us. She always had a hard time keeping up. The fact that Darwin put away the only thing that helped her keep up made her sad.

Megan asked, "Why did you put that away? Wouldn't it be easier to drive that to the location?"

Darwin said, "We can't see well with it and I'm running low on mana. Also, the dwarves may attack us if they see something like that. They are engineers that are the best in this world. I'm sure the dwarves have something far superior to what I got."

Megan didn't believe him in the second part but believed he was low on mana from the first part. Creating something takes lots of mana. I just didn't care. We needed to walk. I was beginning to get out of shape. My body was feeling like the mana was being drained out of me most of the time.

We could hear many animals around us. I thought it was weird. There was no vegetation around here. I looked over and saw a snake wrapping itself around a small rabbit. The snake was big enough to crush a human. I'm so glad that it wasn't me snake was after. I tried to ignore it, but the rabbit was screaming out in pain as the snake ate it whole. You could see the corpse of the rabbit working its way down the tail.

The wind was blowing the trees as the land was getting darker. Chavez created a flame in his hand right hand. Diego and Sylvia managed to disappear again. They keep shrinking and I couldn't find them. I wasn't worried. They always find me.

I looked to my right and saw a few figures. They were slowly coming our way. The figures didn't look human. The way they carried themselves. I originally thought that they were elven, but the elves didn't walk that way.

I could sense a dark aura coming from them. I began to breathe heavily. Something was drawing me toward the beasts. I didn't have the skill Beast Command so it was some sort of beast I could control it. The dark aura looked incredibly strong.

Michael was sniffing out something. Nobody else seemed to notice. Michael had a look of fear and hatred at the same time. He swallowed hard. Michael's eyes turned purple. As the thirteen figures came closer to us.

Michael grew fangs and began forming red scales on his body. I said, "Snap out of it what is wrong."

Paine looked back and noticed that his horns were starting to grow. Michael growled a bit as purple blood formed in his mouth. I had no idea what was freaking him out. Lightning was formed around his body. It was so strong that everyone had to back away.

Paine opened a portal to the Void Storage. He was worried as well. He was trying to reduce casualties. The intensity in those two is insane. I looked around and there was no Loraine or Matilda. I had no idea where they went.

Paine pointed to the portal and said, "Everyone get inside."

Megan, Onyx, Darwin, and Chavez had no choice but to get in. I stood my ground. Lucas stood in front of me. Blood was coming out of his fingertips. He was getting ready to go on the assault. The blood was spreading and the land went from black to red.

Lucas turned his hand into sharp blades. He whipped his hands down by his side. Lucas kept looking back at me. He was nodding his head at the portal for me to enter, but I refused. I wasn't going to miss out on whatever was happening here.

Diego growled in the direction of the dark figures. I was working up the energy to use Predator and rip whatever it was apart. As they got closer, I noticed the level on one of them. It was over a level one million. I couldn't believe it. My scan must be messed up. That is a god-tier level.

A force came out of nowhere and hit Paine in the face. He was knocked to the ground. Paine used a Barrier to protect himself. I never seen him use one for protective reasons. The barrier was going down so fast that I wasn't sure what was hitting him.

Michael grew out his horns and formed his swords. He disappeared again and all I could see was purple sparks coming from the sky. The blasts were shaking the trees. Their power was so strong that it was ripping the trees out of their roots.

What the fuck did we get ourselves into?

Chapter 18

I sent Diego and Sylvia out to attack the targets, but they were so fast that they couldn't even see them. The weird part was when I sent them out. They popped out of my hands. I just had to ignore that part and focus on the battle.

The darkness was working as a friend to the figures. The forest began to fill with a fog that was cold and killing the cold-blooded animals. The animals in the forests screamed in pain.

The figures appeared before us. There were twelve beings behind a vampire-looking man. The twelve beings had their Hell Armor skills on. Each one had purple running their the cracks in the armor as well.

The vampire-looking guy walked forward. His eyes were red with black spirals on the inside. His skin was purple and had fangs that went past his lip. There appeared to be no wrinkles on his face. He had a black and gold long coat that went down to his knees. His shirt had a weird design that looked Chinese. His boots were laced up to his knees and his fingernails were black and long. His lips were a dark purple.

The being came forward and said, "Forgive my hastiness. I was just making sure you were strong. You seem to be so now let's talk business. I like you and so does one of my kind. I am Beelzebub the War General of Lucifer the Demon King... or Lord whichever you prefer.

I am not here to hurt you unless you turn me down. I can't let you mess up the King's plans after all."

Paine asked, "What is the deal you are offering?"

Beelzebub smiled and said, "I am glad you asked. We need a few of you to infiltrate high-ranking positions for the sake of the Demon King. The kingdoms have been safe and secure all these years for this very reason.

My men have been killing people walking through here for a few months in hopes of garnering attention. I already have the loyalty of one of you. She is taking care of an errand for me."

I looked around. Matilda and Loraine were missing. There was no way that Loraine was the one that betrayed us. My sister is such a cunt. The king was right all along. This was not going to end well.

Michael chose not to waste any more time. He went into Overdrive and attacked Beelzebub. The speed kept increasing a the purple sparks coming off of their weapons were growing. Swords were shattering and flying from the sky. I tried to stay back from where I thought they were going to be.

Paine yelled, "Don't you have Wind Arrows? I want you to shoot the largest one you can make, but don't put any stress on your body."

Why was he worried about me putting stress on my body? I pulled back the bow forming a Wind Arrow. This was going to be powerful enough to throw all of them in the air. Diego and Sylvia shrunk their forms and combined them with the arrow giving it more spin and power.

The Wind Arrow was making a high-pitched whistling sound. The group had their sights on me. I was just hoping they wouldn't attack me. It seemed to me that they didn't want to take part in the battle at all. I think he told them to stand down. Beelzebub's ego will probably cost him.

The Wind Arrow was shot off and spun hard enough to grab Beelzebub and Michael dropping both of them on the ground. The spinning from the arrow created a force that both were pinned onto the ground.

Michael's face was rippling. He looked like an eighty-year-old man. The arrow had enough force that it looked like it was having the same effects as G-Forces in a fighter jet. The two of them were trying to escape, but couldn't seem to.

Paine ran at Beelzebub and dropped on him. The arrow started to pull him in as well. Paine was always a nasty fellow who had no fear. He clenched onto Beelzebub putting all his strength and weight into him. Paine gave him a bear hug. He used his hands to make Void Spheres into Beelzebub's back.

Beelzebub was putting his nails into Paine's back but didn't realize that pain didn't work on him. He kept pounding away at him as my arrow kept sucking him in. Everyone was losing control from the power of my arrow.

Michael was trying to get away from the arrow as speed was his friend. He didn't like the fact that Lucas was the only one protecting me. Lucas was very powerful but very slow. He wouldn't have stood a chance against the other Demon Slayers on the field.

Michael escaped the arrow. He sped over to me and held me closely. One of the Demon Slayers seemed to be pissed off. They were clenching their fist as he held me closer. Somehow, it appeared that the Demon Slayers knew Michael, but how. He lived with us and was sheltered his whole life.

I was feeling the heat from Michael's armor and pushed him away. My clothes were singed. Michael had the puppy look that said I'm sorry. I really had a hard time staying mad at him. I really did love the big idiot.

Lucas ran over with his bladed arms out and tried to stab Beelzebub in the face. The arrow weakened and nobody was stuck anymore. Beelzebub flew with Paine into the air. There were a lot of holes in Beelzebub's clothes from Paine using Void Spheres on his back.

As Beelzebub was trying to fly with Paine strapped to him. Lucas took his arms and stabbed him in the back piercing Beelzebub and Paine at the same time. Lucas flew into the air with both of them. He bent backwards placing his legs over the shoulders of Beelzebub. Lucas used his feet to create blood spikes that went through his chest. The spikes just missed Lucas's head by an inch.

Beelzebub flew as fast as he could around trying to toss both of them off of him. Nobody was letting go. Michael went up to Lucas and told him to get off. Lucas jumped through the air and landed on the ground.

The Demon Slayers were observing what was going on. They looked like they were about to attack Lucas. Lucas looked right back at them with his bloodlust eyes. The red was very intimidating to a Demon Slayer. After all, they are still mortal. Lucas could be resurrected every few years. Which doesn't make any sense at all. He wasn't supposed to be awake for another year.

My father must have done something to speed up the process of his resurrection. Lucas didn't even have a face when I came to the battle. I will have to confront my father when I get back.

Paine was being thrust around at incredible speeds but refused to let go. Beelzebub kept flying faster and faster. His skin was like Paine's as it regenerated as fast as it was hit. There seemed to be no end to this demon.

Michael flew up behind the two of them barely keeping up. Paine yelled, " Do it!"

Michael made two swords and stabbed through Beelzebub's back. Purple blood was pouring out of his back. The sword went through Paine as well. They were both bleeding. The wounds didn't stop Beelzebub from flying even faster.

Michael was having a hard time keeping up. Every time he had an opening another sword went into him. The two of them became pin cushions for his swords. He fit in as many as he could. The total looked like ten.

Beelzebub laughed at us. He said, "You just killed your friend for nothing. Do you think I can die from such puny attacks? Look at him bleed."

Paine pulled him in closer. Paine said, "I was counting on bleeding everywhere."

Paine cried out "Barrier" and covered both of them in holy energy. The holy energy weakened Beelzebub but didn't stop him from moving. Beelzebub's chest was a series of small holy bubbles that siphoned his demonic energy. Michael had two swords and swiped at his legs. The legs fell off and hit the ground.

Beelzebub's legs had tentacles or snakes in them. The legs were moving themselves around as if they were sentient. I wonder if this is the same thing that happened to Gandriel. This looks similar to what Michael told me about the fight.

I pulled back my bow and shot a Fire Arrow at Beelzebub's feet. The attack was lit so as not to create an explosion. The legs caught fire and I thought this was going to handicap him. It didn't. The moment his legs stopped moving. His actual legs grew back.

Michael yelled, "Fuck this!"

Michael sped over and swung a sword cutting Beelzebub's head clean off. The head fell to the ground in a purple blood and puss-filled mess. The body continued to move and attack Paine.

Beelzebub's head grew purple tentacles and ran off into the forest. I was looking around and thought the Forest of the Mist must have expanded somehow. It was supposed to be three miles away and you actually had to travel there.

Beelzebub's body wiggled around and slapped Paine. Paine used Void Spheres to break down the body piece by piece. The body stopped growing back. The tentacles were trying to wiggle away out of the body. Paine smushed them in like a sandwich with each Void Sphere.

Everything was working, but when he used Void Spheres on the swords. The body turned to dust. Paine fell from the sky and hit the ground hard with all the swords still in his chest. The fall knocked the wind out of him. Paine kept coughing from all the debris around.

Paine pulled each sword out of his body. It was taking him a little while since he was fatigued. The blood was all over the ground. He looked over and saw the one Demon Slayer staring at me.

Paine opened the Void Storage and yelled, "Get inside now."

I didn't have enough time. The Demon Slayer took out two swords and was in my face within less than a second. The swords were placed on my neck. I had a small cut, but nothing serious.

Michael sped over and pushed her back. His swords you drawn and stared right at her. His armor was heating up as he prepared for battle. Purple blood was flowing out of the armor.

The Demon Slayer removed her helmet. It was the redhead girl from the Void. The girl looked like she could easily be one of my sisters. Her hair looked better than mine. I was a little jealous.

The center Demon Slayer said, "Why didn't you finish her off? She has no use to Lord Beelzebub."

The redhead slayer said, "She isn't normal. I sense Demon Slayer within her. I can smell it. Check out her aura. See if you can find out why. I'm not advanced enough for that kind of magic."

The center Demon Slayer said, "You are correct. I can see it now. She isn't alone in that body. A Demon Slayer is about to make its mark on the world. Lord Beelzebub will be pleased."

I asked, "What are you talking about?"

The center Demon Slayer replied, "You didn't know. Well, it is rather early to figure it out. You are with a child. A Demon Slayer child to be exact. This means you either have Demon Slayer ancestors which I believe is true as well. Or you procreated with a Demon Slayer. Since Michael here is one of us. I think we know who the father is."

Michael looked at me and asked, "Is this true?"

I said, "I don't know. It never crossed my mind."

I thought about it for a moment. The weird changes in body temperatures. Paine and Loraine's reactions toward me. Paine is able to see aurae. He knew before I knew and didn't bother to tell me. It also explains why I kept getting food poisoning. Now that I think about it. I'm late. I had so much fun that I wasn't worried about it.

I looked at Michael and swallowed hard. He knew it was true. We just didn't know how far along I was. I couldn't believe it. I was going to have a baby. This is bad. This is very very bad. I don't know how to be a mom. Both my moms were terrible.

The closest I had to a real mom was Moira. I don't have the personality to be like Moira. Especially, since I would have to give up being a hero which is my whole reason for existing. A million negative things went through my head.

I had to look past all that for the moment. The group was fighting for their lives. I had to find a way to safety. I looked over and saw a shadowy figure coming from the woods. The fog really wasn't a good friend to us today. Every time we turned around a new figure appeared.

The figure was Beelzebub. He was fully healed. Beelzebub had on a new set of clothes as well. The clothes looked exactly the same. There seemed to be no diversity in this man.

Beelzebub said, "That is wonderful news. You are now under my protection. At least for now. It can't be helped. He was to mate with Michelle over here in my plans, but since you chose a mortal like her. I will have to accept her into the family."

Michael asked, "What are you talking about?"

Beelzebub responded, "Demon Slayers mate with Demon Slayers. There are enough races involved that it's not a problem. You just knew that you were to mate with a red-headed woman that looked a certain way. You had no idea that your mate was supposed to be Michelle."

I said, "The girl that was going to kill me was supposed to be your mate. We broke the system and chose each other. Michelle is showing her jealous side right now. I can see it in her eyes that she wants to kill me right now. She can't though since I have an offspring in me. Michelle understands the loyalty involved with a Demon Slayer and killing me would destroy you."

Michael's eyes turned purple. He wasn't sure what to do. We both looked so similar. The realization that fate was bringing them together shocked him at first. He looked like his mind was spinning. I wondered what was going to happen.

Beelzebub said, "I actually came here to inform you that one of you has been working for me this whole time. She dragged your friend into the Forest of the Mist. You could try to save them or you could let them die. The choice is yours."

I still had that nagging feeling that my sister would never allow a man or even a demon to take control of her. She is a cunt, but has serious control issues. This was going to be bad. The forest is notorious for not letting people leave.

A scream was heard from the distance. It was Loraine's voice. Her voice was high-pitched and echoing across the forest. The look on Paine's face was mortifying. That was the woman he loved. It sounded like something terrible was happening to her.

Paine used a Void Sphere and destroyed all the swords. Each sword shattered to nothing. He sat up and charged into the forest without even thinking that this was probably a trap.

Lucas tried to stop him and form a game plan. Paine didn't care about plans. I ran after them and Michael went forward. Nothing was stopping Paine. Beelzebub had a smile on his face and waved at us goodbye.

Beelzebub didn't even try to chase us. Something weird was going on. This wasn't just a trap. I could sense there was something more going on. I could sense that I was missing a bunch of pieces to a large puzzle. My sister might be the key to what's going on.

Chapter 19

I was having a hard time seeing in front of me. The Scan was being distorted in this place. The trees were creaking making weird noises. The noises kept freaking me out since I heard the tales of all the people that were killed by the trees in here.

Paine kept calling out Loraine's name. There didn't seem to be a reply from her. I watched as some of the trees in the area began to move toward Paine. Paine was blinded and had a one-set mind. He needed to save Loraine. His foolishness was putting the rest of us in danger.

A tree walked over and grabbed Lucas. It lifted him up. Paine didn't even notice it happen. Lucas took out his bladed arms and sliced the branches holding him. He quickly fell to the ground and immediately dodged other branches coming after him.

Lucas ran at the tree and sliced at the trunk. He jabbed it with his blades over and over again. The bark was flying everywhere and blood was seeping out of the holes. The damn thing was alive like a human. That just means it can be killed.

I yelled, "Paine! Slow down!"

Paine yelled, "Loraine could be dead! We need to find her and fast."

Paine wasn't breathing right. I could see him panicking. I think this is the first time I have truly seen him panic. He is usually level-headed. The mist might be doing something to our heads. I was seeing a lot more than usual.

Beelzebub popped up next to me. He said, "Marvelous creatures, aren't they? Relax. I'm here to make sure your aren't harmed. I'm a Demon Slayer collector. They are by far my favorite of my children. Did you know that Blood Mages were originally called Demon Slayers too? The humans needed to rename things. My poor Death Knights got the same treatment.

Blood Mages were one of my favorites as mortals couldn't possibly puncture them. Their skin is so hard that no mortal could break the skin. They were exceptional as they stole the blood from others to fuel themselves. In a demon's line of work, that is a perfect specimen.

I hope your group finds a Death Knight. That would be wonderful. I would love to see a trifecta on a journey. The humans call them the unholy trinity. I find those words to be invigorating. The idea of my best children working together for an end goal. It sounds fantastic to me."

I said, "We are trying to kill you and your master. Why would this be fantastic?"

Beelzebub replied, "You don't get it. We are demons. It's in our nature to overthrow each other. Death, destruction, and mayhem. It is all invigorating to us. I don't wish for my own defeat, but if you kill Lucifer. I am all for it. I might even get to have some fun along the way."

I asked, "What happens when we kill Lucifer?"

Beelzebub replied, "I have no fucking idea. Isn't that exciting? You guys are like dogs chasing cars. You don't know what will happen if you catch one. That doesn't stop you from pursuing your goals. You don't see me as a friend now. Later, I anticipate you may look at me as a friend in chaos."

The group was spread out and not relying on anyone else. The group looked like a mess. I got Beelzebub over here trying to get me to explain to me what was going on. For some strange reason, he was trying to make me feel safe. Paine is in his own world to save Loraine. She is probably dead already. Lucas is crime-fighting against trees.

Michael was the only one trying to figure out what was going on. This place appeared to be his natural environment as he flew into the air and looked over the terrain. He saw me talking to Beelzebub, but didn't appear worried."

Michael slowly flew down to me. He said, "Stay close to Beelzebub. I believe the trees fear him. I am trying to find Loraine and Matilda. I'm not having any luck. Can your Scan not find them?"

I replied, "My Scan is blurred because the trees are alive. I'm getting their readings. It's making it hard to find Matilda and Loraine."

I heard a scream echo throughout the woods. The voice was Loraine's again. I was able to find the location this time. The group ran toward the screams.

Loraine was being held by two trees into the air. The branches were wrapped around her wrists and ankles.

More branches worked their way around her. This part was the hardest to watch. Matilda said to Loraine, "You deserve this. You twat waffle."

Matilda didn't realize we were right there. She smiled and said, "You would not believe what happened."

Paine said, "Shut it, Matilda. We will deal with you later."

Matilda said, "Me, what did I do?"

Paine launched a Void Sphere directly at the right tree. Two more trees came behind it and snagged Loraine with more branches. The branches crept around her body and up her robes. Her eyes looked like she was trying to heal herself.

Loraine kept yelling, "Smite" at everything around her. The branches ripped the robes off of her body. She was being stretched out with branches going up her vagina and down her throat. The pain was excruciating for her. Her eyes turned red like blood. Loraine's eyes were being poked out of their sockets. The branches burst forth from her stomach.

The branches wrapped around her whole body like a cocoon. They were squeezing her as blood was coming out of the branches. Paine stood there in shock as he witnessed his love being crushed before his very eyes.

The trees around us were closing in. There had to be a hundred of them. Their branches were targeting us. The trees were fast and strong being flung around like whips. I could see faces on some of the trunks. Those must have been the faces of the men they destroyed.

Paine's body began to change. His eyes were black and forming into something different. His skin was flaking off. It was darkness underneath. Paine's whole body was slowly turning into the Void. It was exactly like what happened to Solomon.

Everything around him was being pulled into his body and disappearing. I needed to keep my distance. I watched as he raised his hand into the air. He was watching himself change into this mysterious figure. The stars were coming out and were brighter than the ones I witnessed in the Void.

A deep voice erupted from Paine saying things that I didn't understand at all. His flesh had completely disappeared. All there that was left was stars and darkness. He kept looking at his body. The trees attacked him and instead of hurting him, their limbs disappeared into the Void.

Paine pushed his hands out making a diamond shape with his hands. The area started to gain light. I had to see what was going on and watched his hands glow. Michael's eyes lit up.

Michael yelled, "Duck."

Michael sped over to me and pulled me to the ground just in time. He shot a black beam that matched his skin out of his hands. It was aimed in our direction. Had he lost his mind?

The laser coming out of his hands was going in circles as he was slightly floating around in a circle. He was blinded by his own rage. The beam was wiping out every tree in a one-mile radius. He killed every one of them. If there was an animal alive. It didn't exist anymore.

Michael after spinning for a few minutes dropped to the ground. He was tired. That move was his Hail Mary. Lucas ran over to him. The Void Form was shutting down. Lucas made sure there was nothing left of the Void Form.

Lucas put his hands in a fist. He said, "You stupid fuck. You got Loraine killed. Your stupid ego got her killed. She was like a mother to me you selfish bitch."

Lucas felt like he needed to feel better so he punched him in the fast. To Paine, his blows might as well have been from a toddler. Lucas didn't care and struck him with everything he had.

Lucas had tears running down his face with each blow hitting Paine. The water had run out I believe, because his tears turned to blood. He kept punching over and over again. His eyes turned red. I was just waiting for him.

I looked up and something was falling from the sky. It looked like a ball from a distance. I pointed at it and asked, "What is that?"

Matilda said, "Not again."

The ball was the branch that wrapped around Loraine. It was dropping at high speeds. I didn't have any moves and my hyenas disappeared again. The ball was huge. If it hit one of us, the damage could damage us for a long time.

Paine got up as Lucas hit him. Paine said, "Get off me. I know I fucked up."

As Paine said that, the ball of branches hit the ground hard. Loraine's body burst from the impact. Her clothes, flesh, and blood blew up and covered everything in sight. Paine didn't say a word. Her flesh was sticking to his back. His eyes teared up. A part of her heart was lying on his right side.

The sky was dry for only a moment until it began to rain blood. I'm sad because she was my friend. And I was mad. Because one again, I always covered in fucking blood. Her damn hair ended up on my shoulders and parts of her skull were shot past me like a gun. I hated this part of the job.

Matilda looked grossed out as well. I think she wanted to wash us off with rain, but didn't have the energy. She was in severe shock. Matilda picked out the flesh from her hair. This caused her to shiver.

Lucas yelled, "You planned this didn't you."

Matilda questioned, "Me? How could I have? I have never been here."

I said, "Everyone calm down. Something doesn't seem to be adding."

Beelzebub showed up beside me. He said, "Chaos isn't it beautiful? If anyone is responsible, I would blame Matilda. She was out there with her the whole time. Isn't that right Matilda?"

Matilda said, "She dragged me out there. Loraine was the one who took me into the forest. I swear it."

Lucas replied, "Why would she go into the forest? We were warned. The only one here that has a motive to kill her is you. You think she didn't tell me the story of how you tried to fuck Paine. You are so insecure with yourself that you would kill to get her man. Is that what this is about."

Matilda replied, "Why would I kill her over a man? I can get any man I want. I am a princess after all. If I demanded it, she would have had no choice but to step down and let me have him. That is a type of power I wield. I don't have to impress anyone."

Michael said, "Settle down. This is a tough place to be right now. We lost someone close to us. Loraine was there to help Isabella confess her feelings to me. She had been a support and a loving friend. Nobody is responsible."

Lucas yelled, "What the fuck are you talkin' about!? Beelzebub over there said that one of us was a traitor. It has to be Matilda! The king of Zahn believed that she was. He told us they suspected Matilda and caged her!"

Beelzebub said, "They caged her poor thing. You have my sympathy, Matilda. I bet it was rough. I'm sure they roughed you up. Didn't they."

Matilda asked, "Why are you listening to a demon.? He tried to kill us. The demon has issues and wants us to turn on one another."

I said, "If he wanted us dead, we would be dead. For some reason, he has an invested interest in the group. The man also seems to like chaos and this is just the thing that tickles his fancy. I have to ask Matilda what is going on. You have to come clean or you come across as a traitor."

Matilda said, "No matter what I say, you will look at me as a traitor. I will tell the truth and you will call me a liar."

Paine was just sitting there grieving he wasn't moving a muscle. He probably should be letting the slaves out of his Void Storage. They have been in there for almost sixty years already.

Matilda was breathing heavily. She wasn't sure what to do. She looked around and looked scared. If she was actually working for Beelzebub, wouldn't she feel protected by him? He is standing right next to me.

I said, "I don't believe she is guilty of anything. It seems to be that she ran away from a fight. Loraine did the same. The trees killed Loraine. The truth is why would Matilda put herself in danger to kill have her killed?

When Loraine was killed she was standing next to her calling her a twat waffle. I admit while someone is dying it's not the nicest thing to say, but there was real danger there. Until we showed up, Matilda felt she had everything under control."

Lucas said, "So it's my fault she died."

I said, "There is plenty of blame to go around. Right now we need to focus on getting out of here. The best course of action is to get home to Tryanon and sort things out."

Lucas scoffed at me. He said, "You mean to take her to a place where Draco will protect her. She will receive no punishment for this. I guaran-fucking-tee it. As a group, we need to pass judgment."

I said, "We are all in a bad place right now. We are all mourning her death."

Lucas replied, "No, not all of us. Not yet."

Lucas turned his right hand into a blade. Matilda had a look of fear in her eyes. She was starting to run. Lucas grabbed her by the shoulder and whipped her around. He took his blade and shoved it right through the front of her face.

Lucas pulled his hand out making it normal again. He had a smile that went from ear to ear. I was starting to think that maybe he was the one working for Beelzebub. There was no reasoning with him. He just wants chaos.

Beelzebub clapped his hands slowly. He said, "Congratulations, your chaos exceeds what I had hoped for. That was cold even for me. You now have two dead teammates. It's okay. They were dead weight anyway. You have two mages, a creationist, and a priest. That should be more than enough to make up for those two."

I looked down at my sister. There was nothing left of her face. She wasn't coming back. Matilda may have been a nasty person, but she deserved better than this. I loved her. She was still my sister. As the days were changing, I felt like she was growing as a person. I know that something wasn't right about this. I don't think she would work for a demon.

I sat down next to her and sobbed uncontrollably. My heart was aching for my sister. Matilda was a powerful friend to everyone. She had her flaws, but we all loved her. Lucas killed her. He is the one actually responsible for her death.

I looked up at Lucas and said, "How could you do this to your own sister?"

Lucas replied, "Sometimes you have to realize the cunt has to die so we can save the world."

Don't miss out!

Visit the website below and you can sign up to receive emails whenever Curtis Yost publishes a new book. There's no charge and no obligation.

https://books2read.com/r/B-A-TXGAB-HVEOC

BOOKS 2 READ

Connecting independent readers to independent writers.

About the Author

My name is Curtis Yost and I have been creating content for over twenty years. I never felt that I had enough life experience to talk about things. As I got older, I realized that having fun while writing was what I wanted to do and published my first series. American Isekai was a two year planned series that is now be writen every single day until I finish it. The books are completely character based on some of the most flawed people you could imagine to save the world. I'm proud of it and hope that when it ends, people will want to enjoy their own dark fantasies after.

Milton Keynes UK
Ingram Content Group UK Ltd.
UKHW010846280923
429557UK00001B/96